MY BROTHER'S ROOMMATE

New York Times & *USA Today* Bestselling Author

KENDALL RYAN

About the Book

There are a few things you should know about my brother's roommate.

Wolfie Cox is . . . complicated. And incredibly sexy. Unfortunately, he has an impressive stick lodged so far up his ass, he's about as emotionally available as a chinchilla. Actually, that might be an insult to the chinchilla community.

So, naturally, I want to ride him like a bicycle.

He thinks I hate him. Mostly because I've led him to believe this. It's easier than admitting the truth.

And while Wolfie is about as soft and cuddly as a fork, I'm the opposite. A good girl. Reliable. Conscientious. Oh, and completely panicked about an upcoming work conference.

Wolfie's usually allergic to altruism, so when my brother convinces him to help me out by escorting me to said conference where everyone else will have a plus-one . . . I say thanks, but no thanks. Surprisingly, Wolfie is unflinching about this. And that's the story about how I got stuck in a hotel room with my brother's hot (grouchy) roommate.

Thank you for coming to my TED talk.

In all seriousness, this isn't a game to me,

and hormones aside, I need to impress my boss this week so the promotion I've worked hard for doesn't get handed to his worthless nephew. But with Wolfie and me sharing a hotel bed, things get confusing quickly.

One

WOLFIE

"**D**o you know what I mean?" Tessa pauses in her dramatic monologue, but not long enough for me to actually answer.

Which is good, because the honest answer is, I have no idea what she means. For as much time as I've spent with the woman seated at the bar beside me, I'm starting to realize how little we actually have in common.

"You look so glum, Wolfie," she says, teasingly squeezing my knee beneath the bar top. "But I guess all the girls like that kind of thing, don't they?"

"Sure." I nod, not bothering to correct her.

On the outside, I'm the poster boy for an in-demand bachelor. I'm young—relatively at least, at twenty-nine—and single, aside from the occasional hookup with Tessa when I've had too much to drink. I run a successful business with my friends called Frisky Business that's put a couple million dollars in my bank account over the last few years.

But the reasons I can barely manage a smile at a pretty girl who wants to fuck me? Well, those are complex.

My friends-with-benefits arrangement with Tessa works because she doesn't ask much of me, doesn't demand answers about why I'm so broken. She only knows the vaguest of details because I've not been willing to share any more than that, but now she's looking at me with a sympathetic expression that puts me on edge.

I don't bother returning her smile, even as she pats my thigh and calls me a grump, laughing at her own joke. Although, is it even a joke if it's true?

I toss a few bills on the counter, enough to cover her glass of wine and my bourbon, and rise from the stool I've been occupying at the bar.

"You want to get out of here?" Tessa says cheerfully.

"I think I'm going to head home, Tess."

With a silent glare, she stands and gathers her

purse.

Shit. That went well.

I escort her to the door, tipping my chin at the bartender when we pass him. Outside, Tessa lingers, shifting her weight as she turns to face me.

"Wolfie." She touches my stubbled cheek in a way that's meant to be sweet, but feels patronizing. "I worry about you, you know. You can't let your past define you. None of that was your . . ."

I hold up one hand, stopping her.

Giving me a serious look, she lowers her voice as she leans in closer. "Well . . . if you change your mind—"

I take a step back. "I won't, Tess. Not tonight. I'm tired."

It's not a lie. I am tired. Tired of keeping up this charade. Of pretending everything's fine. Of putting on a mask every single time I leave the house.

With one last sad smile, she turns and leaves. I watch as she climbs into her car and drives out of view.

The disappointed look on her face should have bothered me. But tonight's encounter was a variation of a conversation we've had half a dozen times lately. She wants more than I can give. She wants normal. A guy who can deliver the wild sex she likes in the bedroom, and who can hold it all together and at least pretend to be okay.

With a stony expression, I head toward my SUV.

I should feel upset. But I've been feeling for months that what Tessa and I have has run its course. As much as I like things staying the same, they've started to change. I guess I'm a creature of habit, what can I say? And the tighter she tries to hold on to me, the farther away I want to get.

Maybe all the change I've been through this year has unsettled me. Who knows? One of my best friends, Hayes, has settled down—with my sister, Maren, of all people. I spent this winter feeling lonely, alternating between hitting the gym and working too much.

My friends and I created an ecofriendly couple- and female-focused line of sex toys. A big-name celebrity posted about one organically on her blog, and then *bam*. Next thing we knew, we were flooded with orders.

Our website crashed twice that first day. We sold out of everything until we could ramp up production, and then because of the attention, media outlets started featuring us. It was quite a story . . . five male friends who wanted to make a difference in the bedroom versus the boardroom. I became a millionaire within ten months. We all did. It's been a crazy ride.

Which means I should be happy, on top of the world. I have a successful company with my friends. I have financial freedom and more money than I know what to do with. But for some strange reason, it all feels empty. Like I missed my calling, but I'm in too deep now to turn around and do something about it.

Back at my apartment, I'm surprised to hear voices coming from the living room. It's nearly midnight, and I didn't think my roommate had any plans to entertain tonight. But when I round the corner and see Connor sitting on the couch with his sister, Penelope, my chest tightens.

I've only seen Penelope a couple of times since last spring. Once when we went to the lake house, and another time when we all went out to celebrate her graduating from college. I drank too much that night and went off on some embarrassing tangent— all but cornering her at the restaurant—telling her what a good girl she was, that she shouldn't settle, that she had the potential to be anything she wanted to be. And I'm sure a whole bunch of other bullshit that didn't need to be said. Penelope is smart as a whip—brilliant, really. And she certainly doesn't need a drunk idiot, a.k.a. *me*, mansplaining anything to her.

"Hey, you're back," Connor says.

I tip my chin in their direction. "I am. Hey, Penelope."

"Hi, Wolfie." She treats me to a warm smile that I'm sure I don't deserve, and my body responds by heating up a few degrees.

Fantastic.

"Join us. Grab a beer." Connor's easy smile is hard to say no to, but that's exactly what I do.

I shake my head. "It's late. I think I'm just going to call it a night."

This gets a laugh out of Connor. "Come on, man. One beer. Penelope came over to visit." He runs a hand through his already messy hair.

I doubt she came to visit *me*, but I don't argue with him. It'll only raise questions I don't want to answer. Penelope and I have never really been friendly—mostly because I find any excuse in the world to not be in the same room as her.

After trudging to the fridge and helping myself to a bottle of beer, I join them in the living room, taking a seat on the chair across the room. I can manage sitting here for a few minutes.

"How's the new job going?" I ask Penelope.

She smiles and curls one leg beneath her on the sofa. "I'm loving the job. It's the people that have been a challenge."

"What's going on?" Connor asks.

Her smile fades and she gives her head a shake. "Well, you know how I was hired as part of that management training program?"

Connor nods.

I'm not familiar with the details, only that she had multiple job offers after graduating from college and that Connor is proud of her. Based on what I know about how they grew up, things have never been easy for them. Nothing was handed to them, and Penelope's never been afraid of hard work. Connor has protected her every way he can, but I know it must be a relief to see her stand on her own two feet and know she can take care of herself.

"I've worked my ass off these past few months, and now I'm *this* close," she pinches her fingers together, "to a promotion. But I have a bad feeling it's going to go to the owner's entitled nephew."

"That's not fair." Connor leans forward and

sets his beer on the coffee table.

"Believe me. I know." Her normally even voice wavers a bit, and I meet her eyes.

They're the same color as Connor's—a light turquoise color between blue and green. But that's where their similarities end. Penelope's hair is a few shades lighter than her older brother's dark blond, and she got practically none of the height he did. She's only a couple of inches over five feet. And curled into herself on the sofa, she looks even smaller. Delicate somehow.

Penelope breaks the spell, glancing down at her hands in her lap. "Anyway, none of that matters because next weekend I'm going to look like an idiot, and then the promotion will probably be handed to Spencer by default."

"Spencer?" Connor chokes on a laugh. "What a douchey name."

Penelope rolls her eyes. "Like I said, it's not going to matter."

"What's next weekend?" I ask.

"The annual company outing. It's going to be a big bro-fest, I just know it. Everyone is bringing a plus-one except for me, and—"

"I'll go with you," Connor says.

Penelope laughs, shaking her head. "Yeah? No. The only thing more pathetic than going alone is bringing your older brother. God, Connor. Honestly."

Connor crosses his bulky forearms over his chest and leans back. "Fine. Then Wolfie will take you."

What. The. Fuck.

I expect the look on Penelope's face to be akin to when someone suggests your cousin take you to the prom. Instead, her cheeks flush and she looks at me with a curious expression, almost like she's trying the idea on for size.

God, just to be the focus of her attention is dizzying.

She's gorgeous with her wide blue-green eyes, arched eyebrows, and long honey-colored hair. I shouldn't notice things like that about her, but of course, I do. My roommate's sister or not, she's a beautiful woman.

This only illustrates what an absolute mess I am. The fact that my regular hookup rubbing her tits up against me doesn't give me so much as a twitch in my pants, but looking at Penelope, who's in leggings and an oversized T-shirt, makes my body light up like I've just bitten into a ghost pepper.

Not cool, man. Clearly, I'm broken.

The silence stretches on for a moment longer as both Connor and Penelope stare at me. My inner *oh shit* meter dings wildly like a winning slot machine in Vegas.

My heart thumps hard, and my voice has fucking vanished. *Say something, dude.*

"I'll do it," I finally mutter.

My roommate rises briefly from his spot on the couch to give me an appreciative thump on the shoulder. "Thanks, Wolfie. I'll owe you one."

I nod and meet Penelope's eyes. They're shimmering with something I can't quite decipher.

For a minute, I think I've done the wrong thing by offering to escort her. I know nothing about the event, after all. But then Penelope's full, pink mouth breaks into a happy smile.

"It's a date," she murmurs, still grinning at me with those mesmerizing eyes locked onto mine.

My stomach flips. "Uh, yeah. Sounds good."

Fuck. What did I just agree to?

But the chance to see Penelope smile again?

It's a no-brainer, even if it costs me my sanity.

Two

PENELOPE

"**G**ood morning, Penny!"

On the list of people I'm willing to talk to first thing on a Monday morning, my coworker Spencer is at the very bottom. Right beneath pushy telemarketers and the majority of my ex-boyfriends. I've barely hung up my coat and settled at my desk when his loud, nasally voice cuts through the air for the second time.

"I said, good mooorning, Penny."

I'm normally a pretty patient person, but with Spencer, all that flies out the window. I don't know what it is about him. Maybe it's that he slacks off ninety percent of the time while I bust my butt for this company. Or maybe it's the fact that he gets away with it, thanks to a little thing called nepotism. It could even be the annoying detail that, despite me telling him multiple times that I go by my full name, he's insisted on calling me Penny since my first day on the job.

Spoiler alert—it's all three.

"Morning, Spencer," I finally grumble back, wiggling my mouse to wake my computer from its weekend-long nap.

Unlike *some people*, I prefer to get straight to work in the mornings and not waste my time on small talk. Plus, I have a lot to get done before our work retreat this weekend.

My fingers fly across my keyboard, typing in my password and booting up my computer for the day. But I barely get a chance to open my email before an uneasy feeling in my gut tells me I'm being watched. I swivel my chair around, and sure enough, Spencer is peeking over the side of my cubicle, his big stupid eyes staring me down.

"Aren't you going to ask how my weekend was?"

Ugh. What is the office policy on bopping this guy down like a Whac-A-Mole? If he weren't my boss's nephew, I might give the idea some honest consideration. Instead, I draw in a slow, measured breath and plaster on the biggest, fakest smile I can manage. You know, like the professional I am.

"Of course, Spencer," I say through clenched teeth. "How was your weekend?"

He shrugs. "Fine."

I blink at him expectantly, waiting for him to say something else, something worth nagging me to ask him about. But he just stares back at me in silence, not so much as a *how about you?* in return. I heave a sigh, turning back to my computer. If this is any indication of how this Monday is going to go, an emergency vanilla latte may be in order.

"Morning, Penelope."

The low, familiar voice of my boss, David Douglass, rumbles from behind me, and I glance over my shoulder to find him leaning against my cubicle, sipping from his LIKE A BOSS coffee mug. Spencer gave it to David for his birthday last month, and I've rarely seen him without it since. It's a surprisingly goofy mug for someone as serious as him.

"Good morning, David." This time, my smile isn't so fake. I like David just fine. Although I'd like him a whole lot more if he'd give me this promotion I obviously deserve instead of handing it over to his deadbeat nephew. *Fingers crossed.*

"Are you ready for the retreat this weekend?"

"Ready as I can be," I say. "I'm not much of a wilderness person, but I'm excited to learn."

Whoever had the idea that we should have a formal business conference at a wilderness retreat is delusional, in my opinion, but I guess that's what happens when you work for a company run by ninety percent men. If learning to take down a few clay pigeons is what it takes to show my boss I can keep up with the senior consultants, consider me ready for the challenge.

"I'm sure you'll be fine," David says, then takes a long, slow sip of his coffee. "And if you need any pointers on anything, you can always ask Spencer."

"I've got your back, Penny!" My least favorite voice chimes in, his stupid head reemerging over the side of my cubicle again like a zit I just can't quite get rid of. "Plus, I'm bringing my girlfriend, so you'll have somebody to talk about manicures and purses with."

Cue my teeth grinding together.

Manicures and purses? Are you freaking kidding me?

If our boss weren't standing approximately two feet away, I'd have a few choice words for Spencer about that sexist remark. Instead, I bite the inside of my cheek and manage to force out the words, "I can't wait to meet her."

"What about you, Penelope?" David narrows his eyes at me from behind his coffee mug. "Are you flying solo this weekend?"

I straighten up in my chair, tucking a strand of loose hair into the low bun at the nape of my neck. "Actually, I'll be bringing along a plus-one."

"Really?" His head cocks to the side ever so slightly. "Who would that be?"

My stomach drops to my kneecaps. *Shoot.* I should have thought this through ahead of time. My shoulders slouch, and I desperately hope my boss doesn't notice the heat creeping across my cheeks.

What do I say? *Well, my brother's roommate volunteered to come along so I can keep up with the sausage fest.* That's not going to work.

Say something, Penelope. Say anything at all.

"My boyfriend."

Okay, anything but that.

David's eyebrows shoot up to his hairline. Honestly, I'm as surprised as he is.

Boyfriend? Where did that come from? Can I take those words back and try again? *Just kidding, everyone. I'm actually not bringing a plus-one with me after all. Ha-ha, got you good!*

Unfortunately, it's too late for that. David's lips are already curling into a satisfied smile, which means one thing and one thing only. I'm totally screwed.

"Boyfriend? I didn't know you had a boyfriend."

"Of course I do," I say, enthusiastically digging my own grave. "Haven't I mentioned him before?"

"You haven't," Spencer says from behind me. "Not even once."

"Well, you know me." I shrug, focusing on the folder icons on my computer screen to avoid any semblance of eye contact. "I like to keep my work and personal life separate when I can."

"What's his name?" Spencer asks with a suspicious edge to his voice.

"Wolfie. Short for Wolfgang. But no one calls him that," I say pointedly. No way am I letting this asshole's bad reputation with nicknames carry over to my guest.

"Wolfie, huh?" David takes another long, slow sip of his coffee.

I hold my breath, waiting for him to call me on my bluff. But he doesn't.

Instead, he gives me a firm, approving nod. "I can't wait to meet him."

And just like that, my boss disappears off to his office. Spencer ducks back into his cubicle, leaving me alone to try to figure out when I became such a big fat liar.

It's not like me to be dishonest, but the words just tumbled off my tongue. It was easy, natural even, to say that Wolfie and I are something more than friends.

Maybe it's because that's a reality I've considered more than once. Not that I've ever told that to anyone other than hinting at it to my best friend, Scarlett. Though I did write freely about my attraction to Wolfie in my journal.

If those well-worn pages could talk, they'd tell you that I've spent more than one sleepless night fantasizing about all the dirty things I'd like that man to do with me. If Connor ever flipped through those pages, he'd be calling up all the local convents to see if they're accepting new nuns.

But feelings aside, there's something deep in my gut that says this whole thing might be a happy accident. After all, Wolfie is exactly the kind of man David takes a liking to. A man's man. Someone straightforward and loyal. If my boss thinks I'm dating someone so serious, maybe he'll think higher of me. It's gross to say, but it's a man's world here at Douglass and Associates, and it just might take a man by my side to help me move up in the ranks.

My computer dings, pulling me out of my daze and straight into my inbox. These twenty-three unread emails make it quite clear that it's time to put the personal stuff aside for a while. There's work to do, and lots of it, so I gulp down the golf-ball-sized lump in my throat, pop in my earbuds, and get down to it.

Unfortunately, I only power through thirty minutes of solid work before a tap on my shoulder interrupts me. It's Carol from accounting, better known as the office gossip machine. Her hands are planted on her hips, a big mischievous smile beaming on her round face.

"Is there something you need to tell me?"

I tug out my earbuds, my brows drawing together in confusion. "Um, I don't think so. Did I forget to do my expense report?"

"No, silly." She swats my arm playfully. "I can't believe you didn't tell me you have a boyfriend. Spill it, girl."

Jesus, already? I guess word travels fast in a small office.

"There's really not much to tell," I say, which isn't a lie. Maybe if I can be partially honest about things, I'll be able to curb some of my guilt. "His name is Wolfie," I say, drawing out my words to buy myself time to think. "He's my brother's roommate. We've run in the same circle of friends for a while now."

Carol nods along, her eyes wide with interest as I rattle off a quick bio of my newest, fakest boyfriend, leaving out the part about how he works in the business of pleasure. I don't even want to know what the office rumor mill would churn up if I admitted to dating a guy who made his fortune in sex toys.

"How long have you been together?" she asks.

"Not long. But I've always been sort of secretly into him."

Again, that's technically true. We've been together for exactly zero months and zero days, which I think qualifies as *not long*.

As for me being interested in him . . . well, I'm a sucker for the broody, mysterious, silent types, and Wolfie is about as broody as they come. Trying not to fall victim to those dark, hypnotic eyes is like trying to ice skate in the middle of summer. Take one step and you're going under. Which is why I've been treading carefully for years.

Once Carol is satisfied with the amount of info she's squeezed out of me, she heads back to her desk, leaving me to hunker down on client emails and spreadsheets until five o'clock rolls around. Another day in the books, and just four days to go until the retreat. I guess I should probably tell my plus-one the big news about the acting debut he'll be making this weekend.

As I step out of my office building and onto the streets of Chicago, the early November wind bites my cheeks.

God, I hate the cold. Sometimes I wonder why I chose to live in a city that gets a grand total of three seconds of summer a year.

Zipping my coat up to my chin, I head down the sidewalk toward the nearest Brown Line stop. It's just a five-minute walk, which, come to think of it, is the perfect amount of time to have a very awkward phone conversation.

Might as well get this over with.

I dig my cell phone out of my purse, swiping

to the bottom of my contact list until I land on Wolfie's name. He's not going to be happy about this, but then again, he's rarely happy, anyway. So, really, what have I got to lose?

All right, here goes nothing.

I suck in a deep breath and double-tap his name on my screen. Two rings later, he answers.

"Hello?"

"Hey, Wolfie. It's Penelope."

"I know," he says curtly. "I have your number."

"Oh. Right." *So far, so good.* "I was just calling to solidify our plans for this weekend. I mean, if you're still down to come with me to my work retreat. You can back out if you want."

Please don't back out. Please don't back out.

"I'm not backing out." His voice is gruff but certain. "I'll be there."

There's that lump in my throat again. I guess this is really happening.

"Great," I say in the cheeriest voice I can muster. Hopefully, my nerves aren't discernable through the phone. "So, it's up in Wisconsin, just over the border. It shouldn't take much more than an hour and a half to get there. And it's just two nights, so we'll be back by Sunday evening. I can pick you up on Friday afternoon, and we should be there in time for—"

"I'll drive," he says, interrupting me. "Friday afternoon? I'll pick you up."

All-righty then.

"Ohhh-kay," I manage to get out. "And, um, one more teeny-tiny thing."

"Yes?"

Just say it, Penelope. "I may have accidentally told everyone at the office that my boyfriend is coming with me."

The line is quiet for what feels like half a lifetime. So quiet, in fact, that I have to double-check to be sure he didn't just hang up on me. But no, the call is very much still going. He's just as silent as a stone.

"Um, Wolfie?"

"Yes?"

"Did . . . did you hear what I said?"

He's quiet again, then finally says, "Uh, your boyfriend?"

"Yup. Good, you heard. Okay, gotta go. 'Bye.

See you Friday!"

The words tumble out at the speed of light, and before he can get another word in, I hang up, then immediately power down my phone so he can't call me back. If he tries, I'll blame it on bad reception on the Brown Line. By the time I step onto the train, I can hardly hear the stops being announced over the blood thrumming in my ears.

Well, I guess that could have gone worse.

Three

WOLFIE

I've almost canceled this trip half a dozen times, and maybe I should have. But in the end, I couldn't just leave Penelope hanging. Plus, Connor would never let me live with the fact that I ditched his sister.

My mantra has been *just smile and get it over with*. And so far . . . I'm dealing.

I've just endured a tense two-hour road trip with Penelope beside me. She smells *really* fucking good. And she's chattered almost nonstop, giving me the play-by-play of the politics in her office. I'm not sure if it's nervous energy, or if she just *really* wants me to be prepared for this weekend. Either way, it's kind of adorable listening to her ramble on.

Adorable? Get it together, bro.

When Penelope sprang the news on me that she'd told her colleagues she was bringing her *boyfriend*, I almost swallowed my tongue. But I had little choice but to go along with it. *Right?*

I let out a deep sigh and grip the steering wheel tighter.

Forty-eight hours and I'll be home. Safe and away from all this nonsense.

Even as it pops into my head, I realize what a strange thought it is. Safe from what?

Feels, I decide.

Penelope makes me *feel* too many things. Most of them all at once.

Confused. Overwhelmed. Horny.

For most guys, that last one isn't usually a problem. Unfortunately for me, I'm not most guys.

Physical intimacy makes me . . . unsettled. Nervous. Fearful about what might happen next. Worried about what's expected of me. Guys are expected to perform. That's just the way it is.

It's probably some type of undiagnosed anxiety disorder, but I don't want to go sit on a couch and tell some overpriced shrink about my past. I know exactly why I am the way I am.

I let out another sigh and shift in my seat.

"Are you okay?" Penelope asks softly from beside me, lowering her dark sunglasses to meet my eyes.

She's way too perceptive, or maybe I'm way too obvious.

"Fine," I lie, focusing on the road ahead.

When we arrive at the hotel, I grab our bags from the trunk while Penelope talks to the valet. She laughs at something he says, and I want to throat-punch him. I'm not off to a great start.

Chill, Wolfie.

The twenty-something valet turns his attention to me. "Name, sir?" He's got mischievous blue eyes, and I doubt *he* has any problems when it comes to the opposite sex.

"Wolfgang Cox."

He jots something down on the valet ticket and tears off half for me. "Gotcha down. You guys enjoy your stay."

With a stiff nod, I shoulder my bag and roll Penelope's along as I follow her inside, through the sliding glass doors of the opulent resort. I've never even heard of this place, but it's somewhere between a luxury hotel and a wilderness retreat. Towering pine trees crowd the glittering glass and rustic wood building. A pond is in the back that you can see in the distance since everything is open concept. It's nice. Classy and rustic at the same time.

Penelope works at a top management consulting firm in Chicago. Of course they'd want something befitting their status and prestige for their corporate event.

"Oh, wow. Look at this," Penelope says from beside me. With wide eyes, she tilts her head back, taking in the grand lobby with vaulted ceilings and a massive stone fireplace that dominates the center of the room.

"Beautiful," I murmur, taking in her, rather than our surroundings. "You ready for this weekend?"

She meets my eyes. "Yes. And with you here," she says with a smile, "it's going to be a huge help. I can't thank you enough for agreeing to come along. I know you probably had better things to do this weekend."

I shrug. "No need to thank me. Connor is my roommate and one of my best friends. Of course

I'd help his sister."

Her smile falters for a second, but then she flashes me another grin.

Let's be honest, I'm little more than an emotional support animal. And I hope to be at least half as helpful as a well-trained Labrador retriever.

Penelope stops at the check-in desk and gives her name to the clerk. We're given two room keys and then head together to the elevator.

"Shit," she says under her breath, her confident steps faltering.

"What is it?"

She nods toward the elevator bank. "That's Spencer."

I lift one eyebrow at her. "Wanna introduce me?"

With an inhale, she nods. "Might as well get this over with."

Penelope straightens her spine and dons a look like she's preparing to go into battle. I stride alongside her like some well-trained assistant as she marches toward the elevator.

"Penny," Spencer says, grinning at her when we approach.

Penny?

I give her a curious look, and she frowns. I'm not sure what I was expecting with Spencer, but it wasn't *this*.

The guy standing before us is barely taller than Penelope's five feet, two inches. He's dressed in an oversize sport coat that nearly swallows his frame. His hair is thin and greasy, about chin-length, and has been hastily tucked behind his ears.

"Spencer, this is Wolfie Cox."

I extend a hand toward him. "Nice to meet you."

"Did you get the itinerary for this weekend?" Spencer asks Penelope while not-so-subtly checking out her tits.

Asshole.

"Itinerary?" She blinks.

Spencer's mouth curls into a smirk. "I must have forgotten to send it to you."

Her eyes narrow. Something tells me there's a story here, like maybe there's a reason he forgot to send it to her. Or he frequently "forgets" to give her important information. *Dick*.

Spencer digs his phone from his pocket and

flashes the screen at Penelope. "See? The whole weekend is laid out."

"Can I see this?" I quickly grab the phone from him without waiting for his reply and forward myself the message. My phone buzzes in my pocket with an incoming text.

No way we're going to be at this guy's mercy all weekend, or have Penelope miss critical events because he "forgot" to tell her.

"Thanks," I murmur, flashing the douche a smooth smile.

The lines around Spencer's mouth deepen as he gives me a concerned look. But that's fine. I'm not here to make friends or impress him with my manners. Fat chance of that happening, anyway.

"We're going to go find our room and get settled. We'll catch up with you later," Penelope says, pulling me away with a tug.

We step into the elevator, and when I take my phone from my pocket, she scrambles for it, grabbing it from my hand.

"*Penny*." I give her a smirk, raising one brow.

Her gaze snaps to mine. "Don't you dare."

We dissolve into easy laughter as she scans the

itinerary.

While we locate our hotel room, she fills me in on the weekend's events. Skeet-shooting competition this afternoon. A whiskey tasting tomorrow.

Good. At least her bosses have enough sense to know that whiskey shouldn't be mixed with firearms. There's also a dinner tonight, followed by a cocktail reception.

In other words, a lot for me to endure while pretending to be the perfect and adoring boyfriend in front of Penelope's colleagues. But I said I was going to be here for Penelope, and I will.

I press my fingers to my temples as Penelope scans the keycard and steps into our hotel room.

The room is spacious with a seating area beneath the windows and a friendly bar cart parked nearby. But that's not what makes my stomach sink. A king-size bed dressed in gray linens dominates the center of the room—looming like a dark cloud instead of a bed. A bed that I side-eye the fuck out of. Because, *fuck.*

Penelope seems unconcerned by the notion that we'll be spending tonight together in that bed. She strolls inside and leaves her rolling suitcase beside the closet.

"This is nice," she murmurs, running her fingers along a small marble table that holds a coffee maker and an assortment of tea bags.

I make a noncommittal sound. Nothing will happen in that bed. It's just that this is the first time I've ever been alone with Penelope—for an entire weekend. It's only natural that I should feel on edge. *Right?*

Fuck. I'm losing it. And according to that itinerary, I'll be expected to fire a gun in a little while—without shooting Spencer or any other motherfucker who dares to look at Penelope's tits again.

Good times.

"Did you need the bathroom?" she asks, eyeing me from across the room.

I gesture for her to go ahead. "It's all yours."

She nods, murmuring something about a two-hour car ride, and scurries away. I set my duffel bag into the closet and find a spot to plug in my phone charger.

Jesus. I scrub one hand through my hair. *What the fuck am I doing here?*

When Penelope reemerges a few minutes later, she's changed her outfit and freshened her makeup, by the looks of it. Her lips are now painted a berry color.

Her features are delicate with high cheekbones and wide, round eyes that are curious and filled with intelligence. Her mouth is lush and full, and her honey-colored hair curls ever-so-slightly on the ends over her perky breasts. But that perfect exterior is only part of the package. She's kindhearted, and has a quick wit and a wonderful sense of humor. Penelope is a treat for all the senses.

"You ready for this?" she asks.

I glance at the time. The skeet-shooting competition starts in thirty minutes.

At my hesitation, Penelope laughs. "You're starting to question why you signed up for this, aren't you?"

"Not at all. It's going to be fine," I say, but her raised brows tell me I'm not at all convincing.

Try harder, dude.

I'm here to help her, not stress her out. *You're doing this for Connor. At least try to be a decent friend.*

With some directions from the concierge staff, we make it outside to the edge of a grassy pasture where the skeet-shooting competition is being held. The rolling hills in the distance are dotted with tall pine trees, and another pond is nearby where we can see wild turkeys roaming.

Penelope ties the belt at the waist of her black wool coat. She looks gorgeous. Not even remotely dressed for skeet-shooting, but gorgeous all the same. She's wearing stylish tan boots, dark jeans, and a bright red sweater.

I'm relieved when she shoves her hands into oversized mittens. It's fucking freezing out here. I'd love to march her back inside and have her sit beside the fire in the lobby. Order her a hot chocolate, maybe.

Sometimes it's hard not to think of Penelope as my roommate's younger sister. At other times, it's hard to think of her as I should. Like right now, because she looks so good, and the idea of sharing a bed with her later is eating at me.

Connor's the one who suggested this, and if he had any inkling about the things I feel for Penelope, there's no way he would have. The temptation is real, but absolutely nothing will happen between us.

Her boss strides over and introduces himself. "David Douglass," he says, extending a hand in my direction. "You must be the boyfriend."

He's got a commanding presence about him

and seems nice enough. That Spencer kid trails along behind him, wearing a shitty grin on his face.

"Wolfie," I say, returning his handshake. "Penelope's told me many good things."

David's smile widens. "Has she?"

"Yes, sir. She enjoys her position very much."

He nods once while Penelope stands quietly beside me. "That's good to hear. She's certainly been an asset to the company."

"Thank you, Mr. Douglass," she says, relaxing her posture slightly beside me.

"And what is it that you do?" he asks, directing his inquisitive stare my way again.

"Wolfie is an entrepreneur," Penelope says, jumping in to answer for me.

I chuckle. "Something like that. I started a company a few years ago with a few friends. We've been fortunate to find our niche market."

David opens his mouth to ask a follow-up question, but we're interrupted. And thankfully so—I really don't want to tell my fake girlfriend's boss I manufacture and sell the vibrator his wife probably has in her bedside drawer.

A guy from the resort comes over carrying two

shotguns. "Everyone ready to get started?"

"Nothing wrong with a little friendly competition. Am I right?" David asks, placing one hand on my shoulder.

"Not a damn thing. Let's do it," I reply confidently.

Penelope flashes me an uncertain look.

"We've got this," I whisper, resting my arm around her shoulders and giving her a gentle squeeze.

About a dozen of us are divided into two-person teams. I'm paired with Penelope. David and Spencer are together, and then the rest of Penelope's coworkers couple up.

We're given our instructions and a short safety briefing by the guy from the resort, and then it's time to begin. We watch as David fires off a succession of perfect shots—obliterating each clay pigeon that arcs into the clear blue sky.

"Nicely done, Uncle Dave," Spencer says, getting into position for his turn.

He nearly shits himself when the gun goes off the first time, and totally misses the target.

"Pull," he says again, his face red with embarrassment. He misses again. And again.

The smell of gunpowder hangs in the air, and everyone is quiet for a beat. I almost feel bad for the guy. Then I remember his treatment of Penelope earlier, and I'm back to not caring in the least if he makes a fool of himself.

"Wolfie. You're up," David says next, his voice stern.

I take the shotgun and get into position, squaring my shoulders while everyone watches. I haven't fired many guns in my life, but surely I can perform better than Spencer. *I hope.*

I inhale slowly and look through the sight. When I take my shot, I'm rewarded with a satisfying crack as the pigeon explodes.

Penelope gives a little cheer from beside me.

I walk to the next station and fire again. This time I miss. But I make the next several shots, and end up just behind David in the rankings.

When it's Penelope's turn, I can't help but feel a little nervous for her. Like maybe in David's eyes, there's more on the line than just a friendly competition.

Everyone is quiet as she steps up and gets into position. Penelope lifts the shotgun and widens her stance.

"Pull," she says, her voice clear and steady. The explosion of her shot follows, but the clay pigeon she was aiming for remains intact as it falls to the ground a distance away.

She missed. I release a slow breath.

"Pull," she says again.

This time there's a satisfying crack, and pride bursts through me. She aims and fires, shattering the clay pigeons again and again.

Over the course of her turn, she outshoots both Spencer and me, coming in only behind David. Her boss looks pleased by her performance.

It doesn't surprise me in the least. Penelope is good at everything she tries, as far as I can tell.

"You were good at that," I say once she hands the shotgun to a coworker who looks nervous to follow her.

She smiles. "Why don't you seem surprised?"

I chuckle. "Because I'm not."

Meeting my eyes with a soft expression, Penelope parts her lips, quietly watching me.

Pride gives way to another emotion. Something

darker and more primal. *Lust.*

Stop. I won't let myself entertain the fantasy of Penelope and me tearing up the sheets in that bed upstairs.

I swallow past a lump in my throat.

When the results of the competition come in, it's no shocker that her boss, David, won. It's become obvious why he chose this place for the corporate retreat. But Penelope and some older guy in management have tied for second place.

Congratulatory handshakes are shared all around as the event wraps up. Penelope leans against me, resting her head on my shoulder, and all the thoughts in my head vanish.

"Congratulations," I murmur past the lump in my throat as I place my arm around her shoulders.

She makes a noncommittal sound.

"You okay?" I ask, my voice coming out deep and gruff.

She lifts her head, meeting my gaze. Her eyes are so expressive. They're like the ocean at sunset, unpredictable in their depths. You know a lot is happening beneath the surface, but you're never sure exactly what.

"I'm fine."

"Your feet bothering you in those boots?"

Her lips part as her eyes widen. "How did you know?"

I chuckle and shake my head. "Just a hunch."

They look new. And now she's leaning against my shoulder, happy to let me support her body weight, so it wasn't hard to guess.

"I think we're about done here," I say. "Should we head inside? Warm you up a bit?"

She nods, and after we return our equipment, we head inside.

That night at dinner, I'm in awe of Penelope.

As she introduces me to more of her coworkers and I watch her work the room, it becomes obvious. Penelope isn't just book smart—she's people smart. She can easily read the situation and tailor her approach. She knows how to talk to people, how to make conversation—both the small-talk stuff that I suck at, like in line at the coffee shop, and the bigger stuff like politics or science—without getting emotional or offending someone.

I'm in awe.

But I also have to work to keep my frustrations in check.

Not only did her misogynistic boss ignore her most of the evening, but anytime she tried to bring up new ideas in the conversation, he was belittling, almost as though he was thinking *let the grown-ups talk, Penny*.

Seriously, what the fuck is with everyone calling her Penny? I know for sure she doesn't like the nickname. But she just kept clenching her jaw all night and enduring it, so I did the same.

Now that we're back in our hotel room for the night, Penelope sits on the bed to remove her heels one by one.

"What a disaster of an evening," she mutters, rubbing the arch of her foot.

"It wasn't that bad. You kicked ass at shooting."

She smirks. "I kinda did. But believe me, it was still a disaster. David sees me as little more than an overpriced intern."

I can't defend David because he is kind of a dick, so I do the next best thing I can think of. Strolling over to the bar cart, I select a bottle of

Jameson and grab two glasses. I know I can't fix how she's feeling, but maybe a glass of something potent will help relax her a little.

Penelope raises her eyebrows as I pour her a glass. "You sure drinking whiskey is a good idea when we'll be sharing a bed?"

I shake my head at her, feeling unsettled, even though I'm sure she's kidding. A girl like Penelope would never be interested in me. "I promise to keep my hands to myself."

Her eyes flash with some unreadable emotion.

When I cross the room and hand her a glass, she accepts, then settles back against the pillows. I take a seat beside her with my own glass.

"Thanks, Wolfie." She lets out a long sigh and takes a sip of her drink. "I hate not being taken seriously. Being looked down on."

I nod. Penelope and Connor grew up without much, and she's been through a lot. As a result, she's driven to overcome her past. To prove herself. And I get that.

Scowling, she says, "I hate when people assume I won't amount to much."

I meet her eyes. "So prove them wrong."

She smiles, her full mouth lifting. "Oh, I intend to."

She licks her lips, still watching me, and for a second I'm sure she wants me to kiss her. But that can't be . . . *can it?*

Muttering something about getting another drink, I scramble toward the bar cart, needing to put some distance between us. When I return, Penelope has finished her drink.

"You want more?" I ask, settling in beside her again.

She shakes her head. "Sleepy." Scooting closer on the bed, she curls into my side and lays her head on my shoulder.

"Just rest then."

She nestles closer, doing just that. It's been a long day, and tomorrow will prove to be even more challenging.

I'm not used to this—being someone's comfort—but Penelope seems content to use me as a pillow, and I don't have the heart to move her.

When my cell phone buzzes in the pocket of my dress pants, I shift carefully so as not to wake her and pull it out. It's a text from Tessa.

You up?

A sinking feeling settles inside me. Even if I were home, there's not a single part of me that's interested in a hookup with Tessa right now.

I look down at the sleeping girl beside me, and my heart aches. I'll never be good enough for someone like Penelope, but giving nothing more than scraps of myself to Tessa isn't fair either. They both deserve more.

I swallow the last of my whiskey and type out a reply to Tessa.

I'm sorry, Tess. But things are over between us.

She doesn't even bother to reply.

Four

PENELOPE

There's only one thing more dangerous than falling asleep on top of Wolfie Cox . . .

Waking up in the same situation.

I'm happy to report that, despite the hard, tough-guy act he puts on, the man makes a shockingly good pillow. This morning, I'm feeling more well rested than I've felt in months. Sure, I could credit it to the high-thread-count sheets or even blame the Jameson I had before bed, but I know the truth—there's something about this tough, grumpy man that makes me feel entirely comfortable and totally relaxed.

I'd be an anxious wreck this weekend if Wolfie weren't by my side, supporting me through every outdoor activity and boring corporate conversation with my boss. Even if our relationship is fake, the comfort of having him here with me is very, very real.

And that fact scares the absolute shit out of me.

It's just an act, Penelope. It's pretend. He's not your boyfriend. Don't get attached.

I repeat this mantra over and over in my head as I hurry through my morning routine—a quick shower, a double coat of mascara, and I'm ready to face the day.

Wolfie, however, is still sound asleep by the time I'm done in the bathroom, soft, rumbling snores leaking from his lips. It's kind of cute, to be honest. I give his shoulder a little shake and he growls, squeezing his eyes closed extra tight before barely cracking one open.

"What?" he grumbles, holding up a hand to block out the sun.

"Good morning, sleepyhead. It's time to get up."

He acknowledges me with a grunt, then shoves off the covers, and it takes every bit of self-control in my body to ignore the stiff outline of his morning wood in his gray sweatpants. As if I weren't already having a tough time keeping my hands to myself.

He may be kinda quiet and grumpy, but the man is hot as fuck.

Once Wolfie is showered and dressed, I slip on a much comfier pair of shoes than those torturous boots from yesterday. We head for the elevators, ready to start our day with two of my favorite F words—*free* and *food*. The itinerary promised a full continental breakfast starting at eight, and I'm dying to find out if there's a Belgian waffle in the cards for me this morning.

What can I say? I take my breakfast foods very seriously.

We step out of the elevator and walk shoulder to shoulder through the lobby, joining the dozens of familiar faces loading up their plates. The long wood tables boast all the usual hotel breakfast offerings—fruit, yogurt, and those little packages of cereal that serve as totally rude reminders of how many Cheerios are actually considered a serving.

But then I spot a Belgian waffle on a coworker's plate and do a little happy dance, which gets a low, gravelly chuckle out of Wolfie. I'm not sure the last time I heard him laugh, and being the cause of that laughter is as good as a gold medal in my book.

While I step into line for the waffle maker,

Wolfie digs into the oatmeal bar, then wanders off to scout for a seat. He only looks slightly uncomfortable navigating the tables filled with my co-workers, but he eventually finds an empty table in the back with a gorgeous view of the pond.

Perfect.

Before he sits, I watch as he shrugs off his black jacket and drapes it over the chair next to his, presumably to save it for me. It's a small gesture, but a thoughtful one, and something about it makes the butterflies in my stomach flap their wings extra hard.

Repeat after me, Penelope. It's just an act. It's pretend. He's not your boyfriend. Don't get attached.

Maybe I should tattoo those words across my forehead, because my silly, love-deprived self is having a hard time remembering that.

Just as I step up for my turn at the waffle maker, the piercing shriek of a chair being pulled across the wooden floor snaps my attention back toward our table. It's Spencer, tugging a chair up next to Wolfie's and gesturing for David to do the same.

My chest squeezes in a moment of panic. *Oh no.* I can't leave poor Wolfie to flounder on his own with my boss and his godawful nephew. Maybe this Belgian waffle and I just aren't meant to be.

But just as I set my plate back on the stack and turn to rush to Wolfie's rescue, he looks my way. Instead of shooting me dagger eyes and crying out for help, he gives me the slightest smile and a gentle nod as if to say, "I've got this."

And he does. My horror turns to pleasant surprise as I watch Wolfie greet his new tablemates, scooting over to make enough room for them.

Even from a distance, I can hear Spencer blathering on and on about some article he was reading in the business section of this morning's paper. It's an awfully corporate conversation for the breakfast table, but Wolfie takes it all in stride, nodding along and throwing in the occasional "wow" and "oh, really?" for good measure.

The waffle maker dings and I pry it open, using my fork to scoot the sweet, buttery goodness onto my plate, then grab a fistful of syrup packets and rush over to our table.

"What's up, Penny?" Spencer greets me, his mouth curling up in a sly smile. "You're just in time. We're talking about the crazy article that ran in this morning's *Tribune*. You *do* read the business section every morning, right?"

"Of course," I mutter under my breath as I settle

into my seat next to Wolfie.

It's not a lie. Every morning on my commute, I scroll through the *Tribune* website and read every business article that isn't stuck behind a paywall. Being a good corporate consultant means staying informed of the market, so I've gotten used to doing a hefty amount of reading. That being said, I haven't so much as opened my web browser yet today. I haven't had the time.

"So I'm assuming you caught the article on that merger, right?" Spencer presses, his stupid smile feeling greasier by the second. "What do you think?"

What I think is that you're a total asshole who is just trying to make me look dumb in front of our boss.

Before I can conjure up an answer that's vague enough to sound convincing, Wolfie interjects with a grunt of disapproval, slowly shaking his head. "Don't even get her started. She spent all morning talking about the announcement that your two major competitors are merging. I don't want to hear any more."

It takes me a full five seconds to realize what he's doing, but then he shoots me that look again. The *I've got this* look.

Holy shit, Wolfie is totally saving my ass right now.

And why is that hot as hell?

"Sorry, honey." I play along, laying a hand on his shoulder. "I didn't mean to bore you with so much corporate talk first thing in the morning."

"I'm used to it." He lifts a heaping spoonful of oatmeal to his lips before adding, "This woman would talk about work twenty-four/seven if I let her."

David gives the two of us a nod of approval. I shift my attention back to cutting up my Belgian waffle, trying to figure out what I did to deserve such a remarkable save on Wolfie's part.

As always, Spencer takes the moment of silence as an opportunity to run his mouth, going on and on about his personal thoughts on the merger. I swear he says the same thing ten times in different words, but at least I won't have to read the article now. He's more than summarized it for me.

Once my coworker's rambling slows to a halt, Wolfie pushes his now empty oatmeal bowl to the side and plants his forearms on the table, leaning into the conversation. "Did you read the follow-up article about how they'll be laying off half the staff as a result?"

Spencer scoffs. "Of course I did."

"What were your thoughts on the salary increase for the CEO that they talked about?"

Spencer rolls his eyes, coolly rattling off something about how it's important to pay our leaders what they're worth, but I only catch every other word. I'm too focused on the devilish smile pulling at Wolfie's lips, the tiny glimmer of wicked satisfaction dancing in his stormy eyes.

"Interesting perspective." Wolfie nods slowly as he tents his fingers. "Especially considering there was no follow-up article."

Spencer recoils, and David's brows scrunch together behind his thick black frames. I even flinch a little myself.

What the hell?

"I beg your pardon?" My boss says what we're all thinking, the furrows in his brow deepening.

Wolfie shrugs. "Oh, nothing. It's just that there was no follow-up article or any mention of staff layoffs or an increased CEO salary. That's all."

Jaw? Meet floor.

A wide-eyed Spencer fumbles over some lame excuse about how he could have sworn there was a second article. He even doubles back and insists he must have read it in a different newspaper, since he reads more than one.

But based on the stern look in David's eyes, I'd say he's buying it about as much as I am. Which is to say, not at all.

How's your foot taste, Spencer? Because it looks like you stuck it right in your mouth.

Once he's thoroughly embarrassed himself, Spencer stammers out some line about using this morning to do "more valuable networking," which I might be insulted by if I weren't so excited to see him and David leave.

"You totally saved me," I say in a low voice, meeting Wolfie's eyes.

"That was nothing." He waves me off.

But it wasn't nothing to me. Him being here has truly been a huge help.

We finish our breakfast, and Wolfie clears our plates while I pull up today's itinerary on my phone.

Looks like I'm in for a long day of team-bonding activities, followed by an all-hands meeting in the resort's conference room. It's employees only, meaning Wolfie will be spending most of the day on his own.

Somehow, I think he won't be too disappointed to hear he's off duty as my fake boyfriend for the day.

I, on the other hand, will miss having him by my side. If I didn't already owe him for coming with me this weekend, I definitely do after that Spencer stunt. I have no idea how I'll repay him for this.

Although I'm sure my dirty imagination could come up with more than a few adequate ways.

It's nine o'clock by the time I finally make it back to our hotel room, a full twelve hours after I left Wolfie on his own, which I think officially makes me the worst host of all time. If I knew he'd be stuck on his own to do absolutely nothing all day, I never would have let him come with me this weekend. Guilty is an understatement for how I'm feeling right now.

"I'm so, so sorry." The words tumble off my lips the second I step through the door.

Wolfie arches a brow at me from his spot on the bed, where he's sipping a couple of fingers of what I can only assume is more Jameson.

He's in the same dark-wash jeans as this morning, but his black jacket is draped over the chair in the corner, and the fitted gray tee he has on is hugging his biceps in a way that's both delicious and dangerous. Delicious because his arms are *oh my God, so nice*, and dangerous because I immediately envision him scooping me up in them, laying me down on the bed next to him, and doing all the dirty things to me that I've dreamed of dozens of times.

"Sorry for what?" He swirls the drink in his glass and takes a hefty sip, downing half its contents.

"For leaving you alone literally all freaking day." I kick off my shoes and join him on the edge of the bed, careful to leave a safe distance between us. "I had no idea that all-hands meeting would run so late."

"I don't mind, Penelope." His gaze locks with mine, and one look into those stormy eyes has me feeling all kinds of things I shouldn't.

"Are you sure?"

He nods, running one hand along the scruff on his jaw. "I like being on my own. And I got a hike in. Good to get out in nature for a bit." He offers his glass to me, tipping his chin toward it. "Want a drink?"

"I'm the one who should be offering you a drink after that stunt you pulled with Spencer earlier."

There's that laugh again, that gritty chuckle that I'd play on repeat if I could.

"Yeah, I got his ass good." Wolfie lifts his glass as if to toast himself, then downs what's left of the liquor in it.

I wonder if he's had a few already tonight. I also wonder if his judgment is as impaired as mine is, despite the fact that I'm totally sober.

"How did you know about the merger?" I shift a little closer to him until our knees are pressed together. "There's no way you read the business section this morning."

"I didn't," he says. "But that asshole talked about it so much before you sat down, I might as well have written the damn article. God, he was being a real prick."

I snicker. "He's always being a prick."

"Then he deserved having his ass handed to him. It'll be a cold day in hell when this loser gets promoted over you."

"You might want to double-check the forecast for hell. Because that is a serious possibility."

Wolfie shakes his head, his lips forming their signature frown. "No way. That dipshit couldn't even shoot a clay pigeon."

My eyes roll on instinct. "I don't know if you know this, but you don't actually do much skeet shooting on a day-to-day basis as a senior consultant."

"You know what I mean. He doesn't deserve to get that promotion simply because of his family connections. You, on the other hand, deserve the world."

A fluttery feeling beats against my rib cage. "Do you mean that?"

"Of course I do," Wolfie replies gruffly. "I don't say shit I don't mean."

My nerves gather into a tight knot at the base of my throat, but I manage to gulp them down.

Say it, Penelope. You've been thinking about it all day. What do you have to lose?

"Um, there is one thing that I really want."

He lifts one dark brow in my direction. "Yeah? What's that?"

My gaze drops to his large hands, and I suck in all the air I can manage, willing my heart rate to slow to a normal pace. I'm venturing into uncharted territory here, but the timing feels right.

I've got the impulse. Why not act on it?

"Remember what you said yesterday about keeping your hands to yourself?"

He nods slowly, caution written all over his tightly drawn face. "Yes?"

"Well, um. What if you didn't?"

It's silent for way too long, and I chew nervously on my lip, doing my best to maintain eye contact. But, *God*, those dark, wild eyes are almost too much to bear.

"Did you hear me?"

"Yes," he says slowly. "But I'm not sure that I heard you correctly."

He sets down his empty glass and folds his arms over his chest, which only makes the fabric of his shirt stretch tighter across his biceps.

Good God, does he know how absolutely irresistible he is?

"What are you saying, Penelope?"

What *am* I saying? Have I completely lost my mind? I've imagined this so many times, even spelled it out word for word in my journal. But now that I'm straight-up asking for it, I don't even know how to put it in words.

My fingernails dig into my palms as I summon every last bit of courage I have. *Just say it, Penelope. Tell him what you want.*

"I'm saying . . . I want you, Wolfie. Just for tonight."

Five

WOLFIE

Penelope didn't know what she was asking for.

That's the only way I can rationalize what happened Saturday night, when she sat beside me on the hotel bed, licked her kissable lips, and told me she wanted me.

Like it was that simple.

Obviously, I shut that shit down as fast as I could. Without hearing any of the details of her proposition, I gave her a firm *no*, threw back another double shot of Jameson, and proceeded to hug the edge of the bed all night. Not because it's what I wanted, but because it was the right thing to do.

And now we've been back in Chicago for almost a week, and I haven't heard a word from her. Not even a text. I'm starting to wonder if doing the right thing has consequences.

But I couldn't imagine sharing all my quirks with someone like Penelope. She's probably so carefree, so uninhibited in the bedroom, giggling and excited to share pleasure with someone just because it feels good.

By the time Friday evening rolls around, the view from my black leather couch looks pretty bleak. Not just because the sky is a classic shade of early Chicago winter gray, but because I don't have a single thing planned for the weekend. Normally, I'm more than happy to spend a night in my apartment, sipping something strong and watching TV beside my roommate, Connor. But he texted me earlier to say he's spending the night at his new friend-with-benefit's place tonight.

After spending a whole weekend away at a luxury wilderness resort, I'm finding being trapped in my apartment has zero appeal. It doesn't help that I haven't been able to shake this tight, anxious feeling in my gut all week. Whatever it is, it took root the second I turned Penelope down, and it hasn't loosened its grip on me since.

I double-tap my phone to check the time—not even five p.m. yet—and I already feel like a lion stuck in a goddamn cage. There's too much going on in my head, and being limited to twelve hundred square feet isn't gonna cut it. I need a change of scenery. Stat.

Propping my feet up on my coffee table, I fire off a text to Hayes to see what he's up to tonight. His apartment is only a few blocks from mine, making him my best, closest bet if I need a drinking buddy on a cold night like tonight.

Not ten seconds later, he replies that he and Maren are doing the whole *meet the parents* thing with his mom and dad out in the suburbs this weekend.

Shit. I can't believe my sister didn't mention that to me. Then again, I've been distracted as hell all week. There's a solid chance it just went in one ear and out the other.

With a huff, I drop my phone facedown on the couch next to me, one hand rubbing the tension from the back of my neck. The guys will probably hit our usual strip of River North bars tonight, but I don't want to run the risk of bumping into Tessa. So it looks like this might be it for me tonight.

Just when I'm about to head to the fridge for a cold one and officially surrender myself to a night of drinking alone, my phone buzzes again, and I snatch it up. Another text from Hayes.

If you really don't have jack shit to do, you could head to the lake house. Somebody needs to winterize that thing before too long.

I reply without a second thought.

I'm on it. Backup key still under the grill?

It's a decent excuse to get out of here, and a little cleanup is the least I can do after all the times his grandma Rosie has let us all stay there. The lake house is almost three hours away, though. I'll have to get going soon if I want to make it there before it gets too late.

Hayes shoots me back a confirmation text, followed by a punch list of what needs to get the lake house ready for winter. He signs it all off with a huge thank-you for helping him out.

Little does he know he's the one doing me a solid. A long drive and a weekend alone is just what the doctor ordered to clear my head. Plus, some alone time at a peaceful house on the water should be perfect.

After cramming a few sweatshirts, jeans, and toiletries into my duffel bag, I pack a second bag containing a few supplies. Bottled water, the protein powder I use every morning to make myself breakfast, and a bottle of whiskey. Just the essentials. Then I head down to the parking garage and rev up my car to head out of town for the second Friday in a row.

I've got a hundred fifty miles of highway ahead of me, more than enough time to work out whatever's going on between Penelope and me.

Is she mad at me? Fuck if I know. I've never been good at the whole feelings thing.

What I do know is that if I was dumb enough to cross any lines with her, she'd end up hurt, and Connor would put my balls on a spike in the middle of Millennium Park. I wouldn't blame him either. That's what you do when some asshat breaks your sister's heart.

Luckily, I'll never have to pull that shit for my own sister. Hayes is a good man. Not that I'm not a good person. I am, but I'm complicated. A bit of a fucking mess, to be honest. And I'm not going to let Penelope get swept up in all that.

I listen to a podcast most of the way there, and the moon is high overhead by the time I find the spot to turn off into the driveway. I've never been here when the leaves have fallen from the trees. It looks different. Almost spooky.

Gravel crunches beneath my tires as I pull up to the lake house, the clock just turning over to nine o'clock as I throw my car in park and hop out. Cringing against the wind, I feel around in the darkness to find the spare key hidden beneath the grill cover, then trudge up the steps and onto the porch. The forecast said chances of snow were low tonight, but the sky is telling a different story. Good thing I came up here after all. The pipes might have frozen if I hadn't.

Inside, I drop my duffel bag and flip on the lights, along with the heat. Everything looks just how we left it this summer, right down to the left-over six-pack of cheap beer shoved in the back of the fridge. I consider helping myself to one, although a whiskey neat would warm me up a lot faster. I miss the bar cart from the hotel last week-end almost as much as the drinking buddy I shared it with.

Leaning one hip against the counter, I pull up the list of tasks Hayes sent over. It's kind of late, but I can definitely cross one or two things off this list tonight. That will tire me out enough to get some good shut-eye and leave me nice and fresh to finish things up tomorrow.

But before I can decide on which task to tack-le first, a hollow knock echoes through the empty house, snapping my attention toward the door.

What the hell?

I hold my breath, listening for any other sounds of life. Was it just an animal? I'm certainly not expecting anyone tonight.

When I hear the knocking again, it's followed by a soft, sweet voice pleading, "Open up, Wolfie. It's cold out here."

My chest tightens. I know that voice.

It's Penelope, which can only mean one thing— I've officially lost my mind and started hearing voices. Because there's not a chance in hell that Penelope Blake just so happened to be in the neighborhood of a tiny West Michigan town.

When I reach the door and tug it open, a pink-cheeked, shivering Penelope stands there staring back at me. Her black wool coat is tied tight around her waist, her honey-blond hair whipping in the wind.

"Hi." She gives me a big grin, one gloved hand tucking a loose blond strand behind her ear, only for the wind to undo her work. "Can I come in?"

"What are you doing here?" I blurt.

Smooth, Wolfie. Real smooth.

"Thought it'd be the perfect night for a beach

vacation." She laughs at her own joke, a low, nervous laugh. Just the sound of it warms me up more than any amount of whiskey ever could.

"Seriously, though," she says, her gaze darting between me and her car, which is parked behind mine. "It's starting to snow. If you don't want to see me, I can just get back in my car and—"

"No." I cut her off sharply, stepping out of the doorway and motioning her inside. "I'm sorry. Come in and warm up."

When she steps around me and enters the house, I scan her from head to toe, still not believing she's actually here. I follow her into the living room and get her set up on the couch with a gray wool blanket, which wraps twice around her slender frame.

When I'm satisfied that she's comfortable, I head to the kitchen to find her something hot to drink. After digging around for a minute, I manage to locate a mug and a handful of tea bags from the back of the pantry. By the time I bring a steaming mug of hot tea to her, pleased to see the redness has faded from her cheeks, replaced with her usual glow.

"Hope chamomile is okay," I murmur, handing it to her.

She looks adorable, all cozied up on the couch,

pursing her lips to blow slow streams of air through the steam of her tea. It just makes it that much harder to take my spot all the way on the other side of the couch.

Distance is a good thing right now. I have to remember that.

"So, want to tell me what you're doing here?"

She lifts a shoulder beneath the blanket, her fingers absently fiddling with the string of the tea bag. "Maren mentioned that you were coming up to winterize the place."

"That's true. That's why *I* am here," I say, raising a brow in her direction. "But why are *you* here?"

"To talk to you," Penelope says, dodging my gaze. "To apologize."

She can't be serious. "You have nothing to apologize for."

"We both know I do," she says, meeting my eyes. "I shouldn't have, um, *you know,* said what I did last weekend. I made you uncomfortable."

"You didn't make me *uncomfortable*," I say, but she doesn't look like she's buying it, even if it's true.

"At the very least, I made things uncomfortable between us." Her gaze is resolute, like this conversation is as normal as discussing the weather. Her bravery is admirable.

I nod. "Fine. I'll give you that. You just surprised me is all. It was the last thing I would have ever expected you to say."

"Why?"

I scratch my jaw. This is where I usually shut this shit down and step away from going too deep into my head. Remember, feelings? Yeah, it's not my thing, but the way Penelope is looking at me, I can't help but give her what she wants, even if it makes me uncomfortable as fuck.

"I'm not big on intimacy, and I was shocked that you wanted that with me. I was under the impression for a long time that you weren't a fan of mine, so hearing you wanted to have sex surprised the fuck out of me. I thought I was just your brother's friend who was doing you a favor."

Penelope blushes. "Maybe I'm a better actress than I thought."

Before I can ask her what that means, she leans forward and sets her tea on the coffee table, pulling the blanket extra snug around her shoulders. "It's not like I'm looking for a relationship or anything.

Just something casual and, well . . ." She widens her eyes, one hand gesturing up and down at me from head to toe. "You look like *that*, okay? Can you blame me for trying?"

I lift a brow. That feeling inside my chest returns because I don't know how to reply to that. I never thought I'd stand a chance with a girl like Penelope. She's sweet and caring and personable, all the things that I'm not. Which just solidifies the fact that she'd only end up hurt if she got involved in my mess.

"I thought maybe you wanted the same thing I did," she says, blinking up at me with wide, pleading eyes. She's eager for a response, but I'm strapped for answers.

Of course I wanted that. Rather, I *want* that. Look at her, for fuck's sake. She perfect. But it's not that easy. I'm not the man she thinks I am, and I'm more broken than she's bargaining for. I can't put that on her.

Penelope clears her throat, her gaze dropping to the pine floorboards. "Sorry. I guess I was wrong."

Shit, Cox. You're hurting the girl already.

"Let's just forget about it, okay?" I finally murmur. It's directed as much at her as it is to myself.

A gentle sigh leaks from her lips, and I don't know if it's from relief or disappointment. But with a roll of her shoulders, she finally drags her gaze back to mine, the slightest hint of a smile tugging at the corners of her lips.

"Okay. Fresh start." She chuckles, chewing at her lower lip in a way that's too fucking tempting. "Sorry I followed you all the way up here just to tell you that. I guess I'll let you have the place to yourself."

I nod, pushing up from the couch to show her out. Not that I want her to go, but if she keeps biting her lip like that, it's going to be a long, frustrating night.

"Text me when you get home, okay?" I call over my shoulder as I head for the door.

But when I tug it open, it's pretty fucking obvious that Penelope won't be going anywhere tonight. The snow is falling horizontally, whipped by the wind and building up by the minute.

"Shit." I gulp down the thick ball of nerves that's tightening my throat, my eyes locked on the snow quickly piling up on the porch. "Well. I guess we should get comfortable for the night, because you're not going anywhere."

Six

PENELOPE

"**M**aybe if I drive slow, it won't be so bad." I drag my gaze away from the disaster unfurling outside and give Wolfie a sideways glance, which he meets with one of his famous scowls.

"I can't let you drive in this," he mutters, gesturing toward the window. "You wouldn't make it back to Chicago. Hell, you wouldn't make it out of the driveway."

When I left Chicago, a few gentle flurries were coming down, sure, but hardly anything to worry about. The snowflakes melted as quickly as they hit the pavement, nothing that gave me cause for concern on the drive. But now, the view from the window is nothing but white. It looks like a freaking blizzard out there.

"Maybe I can wait it out. It can't snow forever, right?" I pat my pockets to locate my phone and pull up the radar. But one look at the all-red screen makes my stomach tighten. "Oops. Maybe I spoke too soon."

When Wolfie lifts a brow in my direction, I turn my phone toward him, letting him see this nightmare for himself. He lets out a long breath, slowly shaking his head in disapproval.

I can't help but be affected by him. His nearness. His bulky masculine form. The scent of his cologne that hangs lightly in the air.

He said we should forget about the little incident we had on my work retreat, but so far, I'm not doing the best job. I fully blame those smoky dark gray eyes. One look into them, and all my better judgment disappears. And somehow, I don't think a cozy evening trapped in a snowed-in lake house together is going to help the situation.

With a huff, Wolfie stalks toward the fridge, tugging it open with more force than seems necessary. "I'm having a beer. You sure you want to stick to tea?"

I bite my lower lip, thinking back to the last time we were at the lake house in June. I seem to remember stowing away a certain bottle of bourbon that my friends refused to drink with me. "Actually, I think I may have something stronger."

A quick trip to the downstairs bedroom proves my memory right. In the closet, tucked behind a plethora of vintage jigsaw puzzles and sleeping bags, I dig up a half-empty bottle of bourbon from its four-month-long hiding place.

As I march proudly back into the kitchen, I lift the bottle high in the air. "Ta-da! I knew nobody would ever look behind those dusty old puzzles."

Wolfie chuckles, giving me a crooked smile. "Where the hell did you get that?"

"I brought it here last summer. No one would drink it with me, so I hid it for a rainy day. Or a snowy one, I guess."

His brow furrows, but the look in his eyes is pure amusement. When I strut with the bottle toward the kitchen, it earns me yet another one of his low, gritty laughs. I've never heard him laugh as much as he has the past two weekends with me. If I'm not careful, I could get used to it.

It takes some light digging, but I find two rocks glasses tucked in the far back of a kitchen cabinet, and Wolfie pours a generous shot of bourbon for each of us. Brown liquor is quickly becoming our thing.

"Should I get a fire going?" He tips his head toward the living room. "I know where they keep the firewood."

"And I know where they keep the snacks. Sounds like teamwork to me."

While Wolfie gets to work building a fire, I scrounge up two unopened boxes of club crackers from the pantry. Not exactly a dinner of champions, but if I don't get something in my stomach before I start sipping this bourbon, bad decisions are pretty much guaranteed. I arrange the crackers on a plastic plate, and at the first crackle of a log, I carry it into the living room, where I find Wolfie crouched over the redbrick fireplace, stoking an impressive fire.

"You got that going fast."

He nods, his gaze still fixed on the flames. "I've always been good with my hands."

His tone is so plain, so matter-of-fact, that I'm certain he didn't even notice his own innuendo. But that doesn't stop my mind from racing toward a dozen sinful places. I give my thigh a pinch through my jeans to chase that dirty thought away.

"Should we sit on the couch?" I ask, trying to steer my mind toward logistics rather than fantasies.

"Or the floor. Closer to the fire." He pauses, then looks over his shoulder to meet my gaze. "I mean, if that's okay with you."

"Of course," I squeak. "Wherever it's warmest."

And wherever I'm closest to you.

We pull all the pillows and blankets onto the floor, forming a perfect cocoon next to the fireplace. Just enough room for the two of us, plus our plate of crackers, which I strategically place between us in the hope of keeping my distance.

Between sips of bourbon, we work our way through the plate, chatting about everything from snowstorms to Spencer, sharing a laugh as we recall what an awful shot he was on the retreat.

But the more we talk, the more I find my gaze lingering on Wolfie's lips a little too long. Maybe bourbon wasn't such a good idea after all, because it has me feeling gutsy enough to ask the question I've been turning over in my head for a full week now.

"You look like you're lost in thought," he says when I grow quiet.

I pull in a breath, gathering my courage. "I'm sorry. I'm just thinking . . . Will you tell me why you turned me down?"

The words spill from my lips quicker than I can catch them, and the shock in Wolfie's eyes is proof that I should have kept that thought to myself. But I can't just sit and wonder all night. Maybe if I understand his reasoning, the rejection won't sting so much.

Wolfie is silent, apart from the long, slow breath that leaves his lips. His eyes remain fixed on the fire, as if the answer is hidden in its flames.

"Is it me?" I ask.

He shakes his head. "No."

It's not much of an answer, but it's a start.

I wait for him to elaborate, but he doesn't say another word. Instead, he stares at the fire, watching the flames lick away at the blackened edges of the logs.

"Listen, Wolfie, if you're not attracted to me, you can just say so and I—"

"Stop." He scrubs one hand through his dark hair, heaving an unsteady sigh. It takes a long, tense moment, but his dark gaze finally returns to meet mine. "You're gorgeous, Penelope. Absolutely stunning. It has nothing to do with that."

Warmth shoots from my chest to my fingertips. I don't know if it's from him or the bourbon. Maybe both. But I've never been called stunning before. It's a rush.

"So, is it Connor then?" I ask. My brother must be the reason Wolfie won't act on our mutual attraction.

He shifts, meeting my eyes briefly. "No, that's not it. Although, fuck, it probably should be."

"Then what?" By now, I feel like I'm practically begging. What could possibly be so bad that he can't just tell me?

I shift closer until we're knee to knee, our faces only a few dangerous inches apart. I'm playing with fire and I know it, but I don't care. I want to know. I want to understand him.

"What is it, Wolfie? You can tell me."

But he doesn't speak. Instead, he closes what's left of the space between us, one hand floating to the back of my neck as he presses his lips to mine in a slow, featherlight kiss.

At once, everything within me warms, and I know for certain it's not just from the fire or the bourbon. It's the heat of his lips as he brushes them against mine a second time, hesitantly at first, then with more confidence as we find a slow, sweet rhythm.

He tastes like bourbon and smoke, the perfect rugged contrast to his tender touch.

Slowly, he moves one hand to my thigh, resting it on the spot where I pinched myself in a desperate effort to keep my distance from him. Now that's the very place he strokes with his thumb as he nibbles softly on my lower lip, exploring how we move with each other.

I've thought about kissing Wolfie a hundred times, but when I pictured it, it was never like this. I'd imagined something hot and heavy, an urgent scrambling of limbs and lips. But this is softer. Sweeter. Hypnotic. I'm quickly learning that when it comes to Wolfie, I should always expect the unexpected.

Brushing my hair to the side, he exposes my neck to the warmth of his breath, pressing delicate kisses behind my ear and gentle nuzzles against the column of my throat. I'm surrounded by his earthy, masculine scent, breathing it in with each quick, unsteady breath. When he finally pulls back, I want to beg him to kiss me again, to pull me into his arms and keep his lips fused to mine all night. And I would, if I didn't have twice as many questions as I did before.

"Well," I say breathlessly. "That was . . ."

Soft? Sweet? Delicious? A perfect moment plucked straight from a daydream?

"Surprising," I finally say, sweeping my tongue along my lower lip in hopes of tasting him again. "I, um, I guess that confirms the whole *are you attracted to me* thing."

"Glad to hear it." There's something different, softer, about Wolfie's eyes, but the tic of his jaw is a surefire sign he has a whole lot more to say, only I'm not sure he will. But the last thing I want him to do is close himself off again.

Cautiously, I reach out and lay my fingers over his knuckles. "Tell me, Wolfie. I want to know what you're thinking about when you're quiet like that."

A storm is brewing in his eyes, more powerful and unforgiving than the one outside. But I don't care if it's dangerous. I want to walk right into it. That is, if he'll let me.

After another unbearably long silence, he murmurs something under his breath and turns his attention back to the flames. I guess it's easier to look directly into the fire than into my eyes.

"How casual you were about sex . . . it surprised me," he says, his voice slow and careful, as though he were stepping on eggshells with every word. "Sex for me has never been . . . *easy*."

I nod slowly, processing his words, then I take a deep breath. "Okay. What about it is difficult?"

He lifts a shoulder. "It seems to come naturally for other guys. My friends . . . the way they talk. I guess I'm just built differently."

That's for sure.

Everything about Wolfie is unlike anyone I've ever met. He's guarded and distant one moment, then warm and comforting the next. Hot and cold. Fire and ice. It's jarring, but every time he freezes over, I find myself chasing the next flame. Which is exactly what I'm doing now.

"So, you don't like sex?"

The question earns me a scoff. "I like sex. But I don't generally do the casual thing. I don't get naked with somebody just because."

"Okay. That's not such a bad thing."

Not my personal preference, but certainly not bad.

"That's not it, though," he says, his shoulders growing tense as he finds the words. "It's more than that."

I shift toward him, erasing the distance he just created. "You can tell me, Wolfie." I sound like a broken record, but I want him to know that whatever it is, I want to hear it. I want him to know he's safe with me.

He shakes his head. "I probably shouldn't."

Getting this man to open up is like trying to pick a splinter out of your finger. Just when you think you have it, it slips out of your grasp again.

I take his hand in mine, giving it a reassuring squeeze. "We've been honest with each other so far. Let's not stop now."

He nods once, which may be as good as silence from other guys. But from him, it's a sign that he's willing to keep this conversation going. He's not throwing me out in the snow just yet.

Prompting him, I say, "So, you like sex, but . . ."

"But it usually takes me a long time to come. I get anxious sometimes. About a lot of things, but mostly sex."

Slowly, I nod, weighing his words. "Well, lasting a long time doesn't sound like a bad thing. Most guys seem to have the opposite problem."

"And certain things just don't work for me."

"Like what?"

Part of me can't believe he's opening up like this, and the other part can't believe I'm pushing him to. Wolfie and I don't discuss things like this, but right now, you wouldn't know it. Despite this new topic, it feels comfortable, like we were always supposed to be this open with each other.

He swallows, his Adam's apple bobbing in his throat. "Oral sex," he says, his voice strained, like the words physically pain him to say. "It just doesn't do it for me."

I try to disguise my flinch as curiosity instead of surprise. "Like, at all?"

"I mean, I can get hard from it. But I never come. It's not worth it, so don't even try."

I swallow, then ask on a whisper, "But what if I wanted to?"

He frowns, shaking his head. "I wouldn't waste your time, Penelope."

My heart squeezes. Something tells me it wouldn't be a waste of time with him, whether he finished or not. Just to connect with him in that way would be so entirely worth it. But I'm not going to press him past his comfort zone. Not yet, anyway.

"Well, I guess we're at a bit of an impasse

then," I say. "Because casual sex is really all I do. My career has to be my priority right now."

He nods gravely. "I understand."

"But I do like intimacy. I like orgasms, and I can give them to myself just fine. It's better with a partner, though, but . . ."

"But you're not looking for anything serious," he says, completing my thought.

"Right. Not a boyfriend, anyway. Nothing with labels. Just someone I care enough about to be intimate with." I glance back at him, and something close to hope flutters in my belly.

"And you wanted that someone to be me?"

Cautiously, I nod. "I'm attracted to you."

He inhales slowly, his wide chest rising.

"Do you think that someone could be you?"

The slightest smile passes over his lips, but it quickly fades, a tense frown taking its place. "Maybe. I don't know. It's complicated."

"It doesn't have to be. We can take it slow."

Silence again. *God*, what I wouldn't give to spend just one minute inside this man's head.

I trail my fingertips lightly along his forearm, watching as the hairs stand on end in the wake of my touch. "Maybe we could experiment. If I do anything you don't like, just tell me and I'll stop. Does that interest you?"

"Yes," he whispers, his voice strained with need. "Might be good. Just for tonight."

"Right. Just for tonight."

He doesn't say another word, but the look in his eyes is hungry. Lustful. Ready.

And I know we're not going to get anywhere unless I take a chance.

Seven

WOLFIE

I can't believe I just did that.

Never in my twenty-nine years have I been so candid with someone about my baggage. But Penelope insisted she wanted to know it all, so that's what I gave her.

My anxieties, my hang-ups with sex . . . hell, I even fessed up that I don't get off from a blow job.

It should have been enough for her to go running scared straight into the snowstorm without looking back. But somehow, she's still here, cozied up with me in our nest of blankets and bourbon, looking at me with a meaningful gaze.

I guess miracles really can happen.

My breath stills as she slowly trails one pink-painted fingernail down my chest and over my abs.

She pauses at the buckle of my belt, allowing me all the time I need to stop her.

But I don't.

Maybe it's just the bourbon that has me feeling loose, but the thought of being with Penelope doesn't scare me the way it has in the past with anyone else. She's as hot as she is soothing, like a mug of tea during the worst winter storm.

My heart is hammering, fast and embarrassingly loudly now, but Penelope doesn't seem to notice. Her hand moves lower, and then she pauses again.

The fire crackles and pops, its light reflecting in her wild blue eyes as she blinks up at me, gauging my interest. *Man, those eyes.* I'll bet they get her whatever she wants.

And tonight, what she wants is me.

I would never have guessed that Penelope was so open about sex. Then again, maybe it does make sense. When poverty knocks on the door, love flies out the window. My grandma used to say that all the time. And Connor and Penelope were raised with nothing, barely a roof over their heads at times.

I guess it makes sense that she's not looking for love right now. She's determined to make something of herself and overcome her upbringing. But

. . . she still has physical needs. Hell, we all do. Even if I don't want to admit it.

Shifting closer, she places one manicured hand over the growing bulge in my jeans, bringing me back to the moment. "Is this okay?"

Those plush lips of hers part in a way that makes me want to pull her into me and kiss her till she's breathless. But I'm not going to do that. Not yet. I'm going to try this her way first.

I take a breath. *Man up, Cox. You've got this.*

"Yeah," I say, choking out the word.

The touch of her hand is electric, and a mix of nerves and pleasure washes over me.

As she ducks her head to tug the leather strap of my belt free, I'm flooded with the fresh, floral scent of her shampoo. It's soft and subtle, just like her touch. My heart thuds as her hand ventures down the front of my zipper, stroking me through the denim.

"Still okay?" she asks.

I nod, swallowing the groan that's building. *"Okay" doesn't even begin to cover it, sweetheart.*

"How about this?"

Penelope's fingers float to the button of my

jeans, popping it loose with a quick tug. My last defense against her touch, gone.

Caution forms a knot in the base of my throat, my usual reaction when faced with any sexual situation. But unlike every time before, I'm able to gulp it down.

"Go ahead," I tell her on a strained whisper. Not that she needs much convincing.

Slowly, her hand eases behind my zipper, exploring, rubbing the hard length of me over the soft material of my cotton boxers. My body responds, stiffening against her palm, and the tiniest gasp falls from her lips.

It's so fucking cute. I can't help but kiss the coy little smile off her mouth, sucking slowly on her bottom lip as needy whimpers pour from her mouth into mine. She tastes like bourbon and bad decisions, and I've developed a taste for both.

As our tongues intertwine, her hand inches closer and closer to the waistband of my boxers, finally slipping beneath. *Fuck.* Her touch is electric. One brush of her fingers against me, and every muscle in my body contracts.

Then Penelope runs her palm up and down my length, and my eyes can't help but sink closed in bliss. A rough groan pours from my lips. Her strokes are gentle. Appreciative, even. Like she wants to know every inch of me. But then she forms a fist around me, moving in slow, careful pumps.

Fuck. Too much. I suck in a sharp breath and, as if by instinct, pull her hand away.

"What is it?" Her pretty blue eyes are brimming with panic. "Did I hurt you?"

I bring her hand to my mouth, brushing my lips against the same palm that stroked me seconds before. "No, it's just . . . you don't have to do that."

"Did you not like it?"

There's hurt in her voice, and suddenly, I feel like the biggest asshole on the planet.

Way to go, Cox. A girl touches your dick, and you have to go and hurt her feelings.

"It's not that. I liked it." I squeeze her hand tight in mine. "Don't worry. It felt nice."

She nods, thoughtfully chewing her lower lip. "Well, is there something you like better?"

God, this girl. She's so perceptive, so quick to talk this through with me. I've never been with anyone like her before.

Usually I'm half-drunk to even get here, to give in to the moment and have a quick fuck. This is nothing like that. But then again, Penelope is un-like any other girl I've been with—not that there have been many. Fewer than a handful.

As she waits for my reply, my thumb traces lazy circles on her palm as I weigh my words. I guess there is something I'd like to do. But I don't know if she'd be up for it.

"Are you warm enough?"

Curious, she lifts a brow. "Yes. Why?"

"Then take your shirt off. I want to see you."

Unlike me, Penelope has no problem getting naked. She doesn't hesitate, peeling away her crim-son sweater to reveal a plain black bra and soft, gorgeous curves. She's stunning.

"That too." I tip my chin toward her bra, letting my gaze linger on the gentle swell of her breasts peeking out from the cups.

Once again, she complies, reaching around the back and undoing the clasp in one swift motion.

Suddenly, I'm staring at a half-naked Penelo-pe, and for the uninitiated, there's not a better sight in the entire world. All that soft, creamy skin and those small, perky tits. I'm dying to get a handful, but she beats me to it, cupping her breasts and teas-ing herself with her thumbs until her nipples stand at attention for me.

"That's sexy," I say, my voice straining with need.

She smiles, then asks a question I'm totally not prepared for. "Will you show me how you touch yourself?"

For a second, I think it's a joke. But then her eyes lock with mine, her mouth curling into a subtle but devious smile. Is she challenging me?

Fuck it. Let's do this.

I dip my hand into my boxers, freeing my cock so she can see how hard I am for her. To my own surprise, my hand instantly finds its favorite spot, wrapped tight around my base. My grip is rough as it moves along my shaft in quick, efficient strokes.

She watches me closely, mirroring my speed with her fingers as they pinch and caress her sensitive nipples, causing soft moans to pour from her lips. Music to my fucking ears. When she stops, it's only to pull me against her, sweeping her tongue over mine in quick, expert strokes while my hand keeps pumping, steady and insistent.

"I want my mouth on you," she murmurs, kissing a path down my neck.

Just the words make my erection strain for her,

but I know better than to let her try. I'd feel awful having her on her knees for me. She'd be there for over an hour, her poor jaw aching. I'm not selfish enough to let that happen.

"You don't have to do that, gorgeous."

But then she bats her eyes at me, like she's the one asking me for a favor. "Please?"

Fuck. Who am I to tell her no?

I lean back into the pillows, my eyes transfixed on Penelope as she guides herself down, treating the broad tip of my cock to a light, warm kiss. A shiver rolls through me. It's been so long since I've let anyone do this for me. It's never worked. But there's no one I'd rather try with.

Gently, she takes me into her mouth. Just the tip at first, then a few more inches at a time until her lips are wrapped tight around my base.

A shaky exhale slips from my lips. *Holy hell*, this girl is no slouch at this.

My thigh muscles tighten as she bobs her head, slowly at first, then matches the intensity of how I stroked myself. But this is better than anything my hand could ever dream of doing. This is fucking paradise.

"God, yes, Penelope."

Not baby. Not sweetheart. Penelope. Like I want her to know that I know *she's* the one doing this for me.

My fingers tangle in her hair, guiding her mouth against me again and again. I'm not one for casual sex, but nothing about this seems casual. It's honest. Raw.

Her lips glide up and down my shaft in a perfect, steady rhythm, and before long, the familiar strain in my groin tells me I'm close.

"Fuck." I groan, feeling her answering smile as I grunt out, "Gonna blow."

I lift my hips, thrusting into her mouth as she tightens her lips against me, sucking and licking until I release into her. She swallows me down until I'm dizzy with something damn close to euphoria.

Holy fuck. No one has ever done that before.

When she resurfaces, Penelope pulls her lips into a proud smile. "Can't get off from oral sex, huh?"

I chuckle and pull her close until she's resting her head on my shoulder. She's so adorable, all cozy and curled up against me. Meanwhile, my heart is trying to beat out of my chest, its version of thunderous applause for the performance she just gave.

"Never have before. I guess you're just really good at that." I sweep her honey-blond hair behind her ear, meeting her gaze. "Let me return the favor?"

I hate to move her from this spot, but I'll be damned if I don't get a taste of her after what she just did for me.

Her lips form a playful grin. "How can I say no to that?"

I help her out of her jeans, and without even being asked, she ditches the lacy black thong she has on underneath too. This woman has no shame about her body, nor should she. She's fucking perfect. All smooth, creamy skin and thick, delicious thighs.

I ease myself down to the space between them, running my tongue through her heat. It earns me a gasp.

She's reactive. I like that.

"So gorgeous," I murmur against her thigh before parting her again.

She shivers and twitches with every stroke of my tongue, her throaty moans mixing with the crackling of the fire in the sweetest, sexiest symphony I've ever heard. It only gets better when she says my name.

"Fuck, Wolfie. So good."

My lips stay locked on her sweet, swollen clit as I sink one finger into her, then add another, until she's pulsing and panting toward her climax.

"Oh, Wolfie." Her whines are desperate. "I'm so close."

I hum against her in approval, and it does her in, her whole body tensing around my fingers and releasing in one slow, shaky sigh of pleasure.

"You're unbelievable," she mumbles once she finally catches her breath.

I join her with my head on the pillows again, watching her sleepy eyes flutter closed as she shifts back to her spot from before, her head tucked into the crook of my shoulder. I think I'm officially her human pillow.

"Sleepy," she grumbles.

As she slips off to dreamland, I stare at the fire, watching the last of the embers fade to black as it dies out. The high I was riding follows suit, fading into a twinge of guilt in the pit of my stomach.

This isn't just any gorgeous woman asleep in

my arms. This is my roommate's sister. And he would kill me if he knew.

Penelope's words from earlier echo in my head. *We could be good for each other, just for tonight.* Meaning this can't carry over into tomorrow. And I'll make damn sure of that.

I'm wise enough to know lightning doesn't strike twice. And I'll never be good enough for a girl like Penelope.

Eight

PENELOPE

I can't pinpoint exactly what it is that wakes me up so early.

Maybe it's the soft light of daybreak bleeding through the windows, or the chill lingering in the air. Other potential culprits include the soft snores coming from the sleeping man beside me. Regardless, it can't be much later than six a.m. when I blink out of my sleep and into the cold, white morning.

From the looks of it, the snow has stopped, although by the size of the drifts, I'm guessing it kept up late into the night. The sun is just above the horizon, scattering its rays over the bright white mounds of snow. It's like a painting out there, a serene aftermath to last night's storm.

But it doesn't matter how pretty it is. It's also

freaking freezing. As my chill turn to full-on shivers, I cuddle closer to Wolfie in a desperate search for warmth.

He stirs, letting out a grumble as he turns toward me, gathering me up in his arms. "You cold?"

I nod, pulling the scratchy wool blanket up to my chin.

His body heat kept me warm most of the night, but without the fire, the house has gotten truly cold. It probably doesn't help that my clothes are piled in a heap on the floor, and I certainly didn't pack pajamas.

Regrets? I have none.

Wolfie shoves back the blankets and tugs on his boxers before trudging over to rebuild the fire. I watch him closely, admiring the way the morning light coats him in a warm, angelic glow.

Wolfie is no angel. He's made that perfectly clear. But whatever demons from his past turned him into the rough, broken man he is today, he didn't let them stop him last night.

I feel strangely proud. And now, watching the muscles of his back flex and contract as he rebuilds our fire, I'm praying he can keep those demons at bay long enough for him to open up again, or maybe long enough to let me touch him again.

It's a dangerous thought. Especially with how masculine and delicious he looks wearing only boxers, building me a fire just because I said I was cold.

Once the fire is steadily burning, he returns to our nest of blankets, folding me back into his arms, his front to my back. His body is sturdy beneath me, but there's a softness about him that I can't quite describe. This man is full of beautiful contradictions.

"You sleep okay?" he murmurs, his lips brushing against the sensitive skin behind my ear.

"Like a baby. What about you?"

He pulls me tighter to him until I can feel the steady rhythm of his heart beating between my shoulder blades. "Better than I have in months. Thanks for that."

"I'm sure the bourbon may have helped too."

A low chuckle vibrates through him. "Nah. I think it was mostly you."

"Whatever you say," I murmur, trying to play it cool. In reality, my chest is swelling with pride. I like knowing that I may have contributed to his anxiety subsiding for the night. Anything I can do to quiet that unease of his.

Shifting in his arms, I turn to meet Wolfie's sleepy gaze, admiring how the firelight dances in his gray eyes. The flames bring out little specks of green that I've never noticed before. I guess there's plenty about Wolfie that I've yet to discover, and I want to know it all. Starting with memorizing the way he kisses.

I close what's left of the distance between us, and he captures my lips with his, our tongues touching in an easy, sleepy rhythm.

I'm relieved to find that what happened between us last night wasn't just a dream. Every touch is curious and each caress is gentle. This man is such a contradiction, my head spins with each new side of him that's revealed. As we kiss, his hand slips from my waist, tracing the curve of my hip with the pads of his fingers until he's gently cupping the warmth between my thighs.

Well, good morning to you too.

I hum my approval, rocking myself desperately against his palm, but he keeps the heel of his hand pressed firm against me, his fingers barely brushing against the tender flesh between my legs. He teases me with soft, lazy strokes, my body tensing and flinching against each one.

Fuck. He's going to take his time with me.

A shudder rolls through me as he drags one finger through my wetness, then begins tracing maddeningly slow circles against my most sensitive spot.

I let out a desperate moan. Going slow with him is one thing, but with me? That's much, much harder. This man is going to test my patience to its limits. My hips twitch beneath his touch, but he keeps his infuriating pace until I can't hold back anymore.

"Wolfie, please." His name pours from my lips on a low, breathy sigh.

I can't take any more of his slow torture. My hips buck, chasing the release I so desperately need. He finally gives in to me, his expert fingers quickening until my wavering breaths shift to quick, urgent gasps.

"God, yes," I cry out on a harsh whisper. "Wolfie, I'm so close."

"Mmm," he hums, nipping gently at my ear. "Come then, sweetheart. Come for me."

No sooner do the words leave his lips than every muscle within me is contracting, pushing me toward a long, drawn-out release that pulses through me in white-hot waves. It goes on and on until I'm dizzy and panting.

Good fucking Lord, that was worth the wait.

"Holy hell." I pant, trying desperately to steady my breath.

He chuckles, sweeping my hair away from my face with the side of his hand. "Not a bad way to wake up," he says with a smirk.

I toss back the blanket, suddenly not feeling so cold anymore, and am met with a gorgeous sight— a stiff erection tenting Wolfie's boxers. Now it's my turn to smile.

Propping myself up on my elbows, I cautiously slip a thumb beneath his elastic waistband, my eyes searching his for approval. "May I?"

He swallows, then nods, letting me help him out of his boxers again. I pick up where I left off last night, right before he stopped me. This time, instead of pulling my hand away, he grunts with pleasure as my hand works up and down his shaft in firm strokes.

A deep sound rumbles in his wide chest. "Fuck. That's good."

After everything he shared with me last night, it feels like such a treat to touch him. A privilege, even. But just as I begin to hit my stride, I'm interrupted again—not by Wolfie, but by a knock at the door.

"Fucking shit." He grunts, fumbling for the blanket and pulling it up and over our nakedness. His eyes widen, blinking with horror at the door. "Who the fuck?"

Frantic, we scramble to get dressed, careful to avoid any sight lines into the living room from outside the window. Wolfie is clothed and on his feet first, snatching up the blankets and pillows from the floor and tossing them into a closet.

When he heads for the door, I'm only a few steps behind him. He tugs it open, and we're greeted with a rush of cold air and a very confused, very bundled-up Connor.

Talk about an unwelcome guest.

"Um, good morning?" My brother's eyebrows furrow beneath his winter hat, his gaze bouncing between Wolfie and me. "Penelope, what are you doing here?"

"What are *you* doing here?" I snap, folding my arms over my chest. How ironic, the unexpected visitor gets an unexpected visitor. Except at least when I showed up, I didn't interrupt anyone's sexy time.

"I figured Wolfie was snowed in," he says, lifting the snow shovel in his grip.

Shit. That makes a lot more sense than my reason.

Connor blinks at me expectantly, waiting for my excuse. I fumble over my words, the nervous energy bubbling higher and higher into my throat. What am I supposed to say?

Nothing to worry about here, Connor. I just followed your roommate across state lines for an unexpected evening of oral sex. It's fine, everything's fine!

Before I can say anything I'll absolutely regret, Wolfie intervenes, his voice cool and measured.

"I needed an extra set of hands," he says, one shoulder barely lifting in the slightest shrug. "Made good on the favor she owed me after I went to that work retreat with her."

Relief floods through my system. Thank God Wolfie is a better liar than I am.

Connor nods, seemingly buying into this reasoning. "Cool. Well, unless three's a crowd, I figured I could help out too."

"Thanks. We could use it," Wolfie grunts out. "I'll get my boots."

Panic attack averted, I exhale a shaky breath as Wolfie stalks across the room. Connor says something about locating more snow shovels in the shed and heads back outside.

That was a seriously close call.

I wouldn't have a problem with Connor knowing that I hooked up with Wolfie, but I'm guessing Wolfie might. He's so private, and I'm not sure he wants my brother knowing about this. It could cause a rift in their friendship, and possibly their working relationship. Who knows? It's thin ice, that's for sure. Connor would probably feel blindsided.

While the men head outside to dig our cars out of the winter wonderland, I focus on the most important chore of all—breakfast. I get the coffeepot humming and gurgling, then head for the pantry, where I manage to scrounge up an unopened box of pancake mix. Fortunately, it's the *just add water* kind. If there were any eggs or milk here, they'd definitely be long expired. By the time the boys return to the house, I've got three short stacks piled up on plates and a full mug of coffee poured for each of us.

"Oh, hey there, Little Suzy Homemaker," my brother teases, kicking off his snowy boots and shrugging out of his coat. "It smells fucking amazing in here."

"I figured you'd both worked up an appetite this morning." I shoot Wolfie a coy grin, hoping he knows I'm referring to the appetite he worked up under the blankets this morning, but he can hardly force a strained half smile before dodging my gaze.

Ohhh-kay then.

Hello, awkward morning after. I was wondering if I'd see you here.

We settle in at the table, the guys on one side and me on the other, and make quick work of our pancakes as we divvy up the rest of the winterizing chores. As much as Connor's arrival was unexpected, many hands do make light work, and he's going to make things go a whole lot faster this morning.

With full bellies and the power of caffeine, we manage to get everything on the checklist taken care of in under two hours. Even Wolfie is impressed, although you wouldn't know it by the permanent frown he's had plastered on his face since my brother walked through the door.

Jeez, this is uncomfortable.

The second Connor showed up, vulnerable Wolfie was long gone, leaving his cold, grumpy self. *Great.*

With the chores mostly completed and the dishes washed, it's as good a time as any for me to make my way back to the city. Connor powers down the vacuum long enough to give me a hug good-bye and a quick lecture on driving in icy conditions.

"Wolfie's scraping off his car, by the way. If you wanna say good-bye on your way out."

I nod, gulping down the nerves clogging my throat.

There's a lot more than *good-bye* that I'd like to say to Wolfie, but I'm not about to risk Connor watching us through the window. Especially not with how wooden Wolfie has been acting toward me since his roommate arrived. I don't want to put him in a position that would make him uncomfortable.

Once I'm bundled up, I head out to the driveway, where Wolfie has finished scraping off his own car and has moved on to mine. A grin pulls at the corner of my lips. The man is sour one second, and then he's sweet. So confusing.

"Thanks for that."

He startles a little at the sound of my voice, then glances toward the window for signs of Connor before allowing the slightest smile to spread across his lips. "No problem."

"And thanks for, well, for everything. You know what I mean."

His head dips in a small nod, giving nothing away. Even his eyes have a vacant, detached look. "You too. Drive safe, Penelope."

A long, awkward silence stretches between us, the kind of silence meant to be filled with one of those sweet, easy kisses he treated me to this morning. But I know better than to do anything so risky.

Instead, I give him a two-fingered wave and climb into my car, praying for salted roads and effective four-wheel drive. Because even with my eyes on the road and my grip on the steering wheel, I'm in for a long, distracted trip home, courtesy of the enigma that is Wolfie Cox.

Nine

WOLFIE

Our storefront is packed.

No, not just packed. Slammed. There's been a line running from the register all the way to the front door for over an hour.

Couples and solo visitors buzz up and down the aisles, stacking luxury vibrators and pink-labeled tubes of vegan lubricant in their arms. It's mayhem out there. But the best kind of mayhem is mayhem that makes you money.

I'm not too humble to take credit for the crowd. After all, it was my idea to start our Black Friday sale a few weeks early for in-store shoppers only. It's a win-win—we get to clear out old inventory before the Christmas stock comes in, and customers certainly seem happy with the lower prices.

"Ooh, what does this do?"

One customer's voice cuts through the noise so sharply, I can hear it all the way from the back office. Not a half second later, there's a furious buzzing sound, followed by someone else shrieking, "How do you turn this damn thing off?"

I smirk at my laptop. Sounds like a couple buying their first vibrator. *Good for them.*

Lucky for me, the only chaos I have to deal with today is in the form of a spreadsheet. With Q4 coming to a close next month, I've got books to balance, which means I'll be glued to my laptop all day instead of interacting with customers.

Thank fuck.

Not that I don't like being on the floor from time to time. In fact, it's days like this that remind me why I got into this business in the first place.

I love witnessing all the excitement as both new and veteran shoppers learn about cock rings, vibrating anal beads, and all the other battery-powered blessings that will take their sex lives to the next level. It always leaves me with a combination of pride and envy. I've sure as hell never had that kind of enthusiasm about my sex life.

Well, until last Friday night. And Saturday

morning too.

I swore Penelope and I would be a one-time thing. An experiment. But when her petite frame cuddled up to me on Saturday morning, all cute and flushed and blinking up at me with those big blue eyes, there was no way I was keeping my hands off her.

Since she pulled out of the lake house's gravel driveway Saturday afternoon, we've only exchanged a few texts, and it's all I can do to keep from falling into a guilty spiral over the whole thing. For the past three days, not once have I looked Connor in the eye without feeling like the world's biggest fuckup. Which is sort of a big problem, seeing as we live in the same apartment and run a company together.

"Jesus, it's a fucking zoo out there."

Speak of the devil and he shall appear.

Connor stumbles into the back office, wiping sweat from his brow with the side of his hand. "You're lucky you get to stay out of this, Cox."

I scoff. "Would you rather crunch numbers instead?"

Silence.

I thought not.

Connor is the world's biggest people person and therefore the best salesman we've got, but I'd bet half a paycheck I could stump him with a word problem meant for fifth graders. Needless to say, the dude has never looked at a spreadsheet for any reason other than to complain about it.

In my peripheral vision, I watch as he wanders over to the minifridge, grabs a can of flavored sparkling water, then collapses into the office chair opposite my desk.

As if I weren't already having a hard time focusing on our books, now I've got to do it with the company of the guy whose sister I can't stop thinking about getting my mouth on again.

I frown at him from behind my laptop. "Shouldn't you be on the floor?"

He snorts, taking a good long swig of his drink. "Doing what, making sales? Your forty-percent-off idea is doing the work for me. Plus, Caleb and Hayes are on the registers, so I can chill for a minute."

My stomach churns, all my nerves suddenly on high alert to his every move. Here's hoping Connor is being literal about that minute. But based on the way he's leaning back in that chair, I'd say he's planning to stay put for a while. Just my luck.

"So, guess what?"

I can feel his eyes hot on me, expecting my reply, but I keep my gaze on my screen. Maybe he'll take the silence as a hint.

Surprise, surprise, he doesn't.

"Hello? I said guess what?"

With a huff, I close my laptop. "Sorry, I'm a little stressed right now."

That's not a lie. I'm drowning in all the work I need to get done today. And yes, I also happen to be a little on edge about trying to navigate a conversation with my roommate after I had my dick in his sister's mouth this weekend. But I'm going to go ahead and leave that part out.

"What's up?" I ask, feigning some level of interest.

"Penelope is in the final two for that promotion," Connor says, fighting off a proud smile.

I lift a brow, urging him to go on. This actually is something I'm interested in.

"It's officially between her and that other dude, the boss's son or cousin or whatever," he says, a deep furrow appearing between his eyebrows. "Do you know who I'm talking about?"

"Spencer. Boss's nephew. I met him at the retreat. Real jackass."

Connor snaps his fingers. "Yeah, that's the one. I guess her boss officially told them this morning that everyone else in the management program is out of the running. Pretty cool, huh?"

I nod, reopening my laptop. "Yeah, good for her."

Here's hoping my screen blocks the fact that I'm smiling like a fucking idiot. I'm so proud of that girl. She's going to beat out Spencer for this promotion, no question about it.

"Thanks again for going with her to that retreat." Connor rambles on, seemingly oblivious to what the mention of Penelope has done to me. "From the sound of it, this company she's working for is a regular sausage fest. I'm sure having you there was a lifesaver."

"For sure."

"What was that weekend like, anyway? Did you have fun? Or was it weird?"

My heart responds faster than I can, thumping furiously.

Why would he bring that up? Did Penelope tell him something I should know about?

In a moment of God-level timing, Caleb bursts into the back office, looking like he just ran a half marathon. "Dude, we need you out there," he barks at Connor. "Put your sissy water down and let's go."

"It's not sissy water," Connor grumbles, chugging what's left of his lemon-flavored beverage before tossing it like a three-pointer into the recycling bin. "Catch you later, man."

Relief hits me like a tidal wave, but I don't let any of it show. Instead, I give him a halfhearted wave, dodging his gaze as usual. "Later."

With the office to myself again, I should be dialing back into these spreadsheets. Instead, I find myself reaching for my phone and pulling up Penelope's number.

Just one text. That's all. Just to congratulate her on this next step toward the promotion.

Nothing flirty or suggestive. No signs that I haven't been able to shake the memory of her pouty pink lips sliding up and down my cock, or the way she moaned my name when I had her all wet and worked up.

Shit. I need to reel myself in. Is this how normal people feel about sex? Because this shit is fucking crazy.

I keep my text short and to the point, tossing in a jab at her asshole coworker for good measure.

Connor told me it's down to you and that shithead Spencer for the promotion. Congrats. I know you're gonna get it.

As soon as I hit SEND, I shove my phone back into my pocket. It's not like she'll text me right back, anyway. She's working. Which is what I should be doing too. But I barely have time to locate last quarter's expense reports before my pocket buzzes again. It's her.

Thanks. :) Come over for dinner tonight? I never properly thanked you for enduring that work retreat with me. I owe you a decent meal, at the very least.

I stare blankly at my screen, restraining myself from suggesting that, if anything, I owe her a thank-you for what she did for me on Friday night. No need to turn this conversation sexual in the middle of a workday.

It's just dinner, Cox. Not an invite into her bed.

Before I can formulate a response, my phone lights up with a second text from her.

Unless you had other plans?

As if anything I had on the calendar for the evening could be more interesting than seeing her. My fingers fly across my keyboard, typing out my reply.

I'm free. See you tonight.

She sends back a smiley-face emoji, a reminder of her address, and a suggestion that I head over around seven.

I spend the second half of the workday fidgeting at my desk, unable to focus on anything for longer than a few minutes at a time. I'm too preoccupied with tonight and overanalyzing what it means that Penelope invited me over.

Does she want to pick up where we left off before her brother interrupted us on Saturday morning? Or is this really nothing more than a thank-you for my fake-boyfriend services?

By the time five o'clock rolls around, the crowd of shoppers has died down to a manageable size, so I don't feel like a huge jackass for not sticking around to help. Still, I opt to exit through the back door rather than out front. I don't need any of my friends holding me up with questions about my plans for the night. Time to rush home, take my second shower of the day, and get ready for the evening.

It's just dinner. Nothing else.

But I slip a condom into my wallet, just in case.

Ten

PENELOPE

In the past week and a half, I've learned a lot about Wolfie Cox.

I've learned how steady and comforting his heartbeat feels against my cheek when I'm lying on his chest, and the way it speeds up when my fingers lace with his. I've learned how he tastes first thing in the morning, his lips pressing sleepily to mine. I've learned what makes him anxious and what turns him on, sparking that dangerous flicker in his stormy eyes. He's let me see a deeper, softer side of him that very few have seen before. A side that I'm drawn to like a moth to a flame.

But none of this intimate knowledge of him is doing me any good right now. As I stare blankly into my pantry, I'm realizing the downside of skipping straight to the heavy stuff. I haven't managed to learn a single thing this man likes to eat.

I close the pantry door with a frustrated groan. *Why haven't I asked any of the easy questions?*

For example, what's your favorite color? What's your favorite movie? If you pretended to be a girl's boyfriend for a weekend to impress her boss, what would you want her to cook you as a thank-you? You know, the usual stuff.

I reach for my phone, hoping that something in our texts will give me some sort of clue. Has he at any point even hinted at a food he likes? Or mentioned what kind of takeout he was ordering?

It takes all of ten seconds to scroll to the top of our existing conversations without finding anything helpful.

Well. That did approximately nothing.

I pocket my phone, trying to refocus on the pantry instead of the taunting green numbers on the oven clock. It's six fifteen, only forty-five minutes until Wolfie arrives.

I guess I could call Connor and ask him what his roommate's favorite foods are, but that would be opening the floodgates on a million and one questions, none of which I have an answer to. Because the truth is, aside from eating whatever it is I finally decide to cook, I don't know exactly what's going to happen with Wolfie tonight.

If it were only up to me, we'd be finishing what we started at the lake house before we were so rudely interrupted by my brother. But with Wolfie, there are no guarantees. Only hopeful expectations. And tonight, what I'm hoping more than anything is that he'll open up to me more. If this dinner snafu has taught me anything, it's that there's still a lot for me to learn about this man.

Just when I'm ready to throw in the towel and order a pizza, I spy two boxes of penne tucked in the far back of the pantry.

Thank God. Everybody likes pasta. And if they don't, I honestly don't trust them. I bring a pot of water to a boil on the stove, then locate all the ingredients in my fridge for homemade alfredo. And what kind of monster doesn't like alfredo sauce?

By the time the glowing green numbers on the oven flash seven o'clock, the sauce is simmering on the stove, the table is set with wine, bread, and two plates of penne. Not bad for a last-minute dinner date. It takes a few tries to get my smart speaker to respond to me, but soft acoustic music eventually fills my tiny apartment, setting the perfect mood.

That mood is instantly interrupted, however,

by the motorized buzz of the intercom, announcing Wolfie's arrival. Just the sound of it makes my stomach go full track-and-field star and high-jump into my throat.

Jeez. I guess I was too busy feeling frustrated about dinner that I hardly noticed how on edge my nerves have been.

With a deep breath, I press the button to buzz my guest in and try to tamp down the jitters in my belly. Moments later, I hear the muffled trudge of him coming up the stairs, followed by three quick knocks at my door.

"Coming!" With one last check of my reflection in the microwave, I head for the door and let him in.

Maybe it's the way his coat is zipped all the way up to his chin to block out the cold, or maybe it's the mysterious soothing effect those stormy eyes have on me. But one look at Wolfie standing in my doorway and everything—my nerves, my frustration about cooking dinner, all of it—instantly tumbles away. As for Wolfie, when his eyes meet mine, his usual scowl gives way to the barest hint of a smile.

"Since when does winter start in November?" he says, shuddering for effect.

"Since forever. This is Chicago."

I slink away from the door frame and he follows me inside, careful to take off his snowy leather boots while still on the welcome mat. God bless him for that. I just cleaned these floors. Under his coat, he has on dark-washed jeans and a soft-looking gray sweater with the sleeves pushed up to the elbows. It's precisely the same shade as his eyes.

"Smells great in here." He slings his jacket over a free hook on my coat rack, scanning my apartment with curious eyes. "Looks great too."

"Thanks. I hope you like pasta."

He lifts a brow. "Doesn't everyone like pasta?"

"My thoughts exactly."

As I lead him into the kitchen, he continues to take in his surroundings, his gaze pausing on some of the more unique elements of my apartment—my antique bookcase overflowing with mystery novels, the stepstool I keep in the corner to help me change light bulbs and reach things on the top shelves. All normal, everyday things for me, but Wolfie looks at them like artifacts in a museum.

"This place is so . . . you," he says finally, running his fingers along the label of my whiskey bottle turned flower vase. "Love it."

"Then maybe you should come by more often." The words tumble off my lips so naturally, I almost don't realize how flirty I'm being. "I mean, you're welcome anytime.

Wolfie smiles, his eyes meeting mine. "What's on the menu for tonight?"

"Not whiskey, for once," I tease, and it earns me one of his signature throaty laughs. "I made pasta. And there's wine too. Although I'm not sure that rosé pairs with alfredo, but it's all I had."

His eyes narrow, one dark brow arching toward the stove. "You made homemade pasta sauce?"

"Of course. I couldn't invite you over for a home-cooked meal and serve you something out of a jar." I gnaw on my lip, readying myself for his usual biting commentary, but instead, his mouth pulls into an easy smile.

"Damn. You're fucking cute."

Holy crap. Never has my heart squeezed so tight as it did at the way he said that, so plain and straightforward, like he was stating a matter of pure fact. The sky is blue, water is wet, and Wolfie Cox thinks I'm fucking cute.

Maybe tonight will go the way I want it to after all.

With plates in hand, I lead Wolfie to the stove to serve himself the sauce. While I watch, he drizzles two big spoonfuls onto his pasta.

"You've been hiding the fact you can cook from me. This looks awesome," he says with a smile.

I grin, then do the same, ladling sauce onto my plate before joining him at the table. We easily fall into comfortable chitchat, discussing something idiotic my brother did at the store today, the conversation naturally shifting toward the topic of work.

"You should've seen how busy the store was today." Wolfie pierces a penne noodle with his fork, shaking his head in disbelief. "I haven't seen it that packed since we first launched the Joie de Vivre."

"What's the Joie de Vivre?"

"Our bestselling couples' vibrator. Patented design. They fly off the shelves."

I gulp down the urge to ask him if he's ever tried it. Or better yet, if he'd like to try it with me.

Easy, Penelope. One thing at a time. He's not as casual about sex as you are.

"Forget about me, though," Wolfie says, interrupting my train of thought as he lifts his wineglass. "Congrats again on your big news today."

Although I'm skeptical about toasting a promotion I haven't secured yet, I clink my glass against his. "I hope we're not jinxing it," I murmur into my wine as I take a sip.

Wolfie scoffs. "No way. Not when Spencer already jinxed it for himself by being the world's biggest douche." He pauses to taste his wine, then adds, "That is, assuming he hasn't surprised us all by pulling his head out of his ass."

"Oh, rest assured, he has *not.* In fact, just wait till I tell you what he did today."

I launch into the story of today's office nightmare, in which Spencer took full credit for a project I slaved over for weeks. As I dramatically reenact our meeting with David, I worry that I'm rambling, but Wolfie seems interested, nodding along and wincing at all the cringe-worthy parts.

"If that jerk doesn't get the ax when you get this promotion, I swear," he mutters once I've finished the story. "Sorry you have to deal with this shit."

"All thanks to nepotism," I say with a sigh. "There's a lot David is willing to turn a blind eye to. So we'll see how things shake out."

Wolfie's chin dips in a firm nod. "I look forward to hearing about it."

"Yeah?" My fork clatters as I set it down on my now empty plate. "You don't mind me yammering on about work?"

He shakes his head. "I love it. You care about it, and I like listening." There's a pause, then he adds under his breath, "Especially to you."

We lock eyes, and my breathing stalls. Every fiber of my being is urging me to lean over the table and kiss him.

But would that be too much? Or worse yet, would it not be enough? There's a very real chance that if I kiss him again, I'll just want more. And I'm not sure he's ready for that yet.

Before I can make up my mind, Wolfie breaks our gaze, pushing up from his chair. "Can I get started on the dishes?"

I audibly sigh. "Sure."

Never in my life have I been so disappointed to have a man volunteering to do chores.

We spend the next half hour working in tandem to get the kitchen clean—him washing dishes, me drying them, then both of us finishing what's left of the rosé. When Wolfie rises from the couch, saying something about it getting late, I know I have no choice but to buck up and broach the subject.

"Before you go . . ."

I reach out to stop him, my fingers brushing against the crook of his elbow. He freezes, pivoting back toward me, but I keep my hand there. I want to touch him. Even if just like this.

"Can we talk about last weekend?"

He swallows hard, his eyes darkening before he averts his gaze. "What do you want to talk about?"

"You know. What happened between us. I just want to be sure you don't, you know. Have any regrets."

He's quiet for too long. I can sense him shrinking away from me, pulling back.

Is he ashamed? Or worse, is he going to pretend that nothing ever happened?

The longer he stares at the floor, the more I feel like I'm about to break. But then a low, breathy chuckle comes out, and he slowly shakes his head, raking his fingers through his chestnut-brown hair.

"I don't regret any of it." The words are directed at my kitchen tile at first, but then his eyes meet mine, a spark of something warm and genuine dancing in them. "Not a single thing."

Relief rushes through me at a dizzying speed.

"Really?"

Wolfie shifts closer to me, his fingers brushing my hair behind my ear, then slowly tracing down my cheek. "Yes, really."

He trails a thumb along my lower lip, then leans in and presses a kiss there instead. Then another. And another.

Soon, I'm lost in him again, pressed up on my tiptoes, reaching for every bit of him he'll allow me to take.

Eleven

WOLFIE

When it comes to women, not much comes naturally to me, but kissing Penelope feels like second nature.

The moment her mouth meets mine, my hand curls possessively around her hip, and the other weaves into her soft blond waves as her tongue flirts with mine. It's pure instinct, as natural as breathing. And I'd like to do it just as often.

My fingers trace the soft, silky fabric of her dress as I deepen our kiss, nipping and sucking on her lower lip. She tastes sweet from the rosé. I could get drunk on this girl in a hurry, if I'm not careful.

Penelope hums her approval against my lips. With one hand planted against my chest, she presses even higher onto her toes, trying to close any remaining distance between us.

Our height difference doesn't do us a ton of favors in terms of kissing standing up, which of course gives my dick the brilliant idea that we should be lying down. In her bed. Where I could strip her out of that dress and give every square inch of her the attention it deserves.

We've done this before, at the lake house. Why not give it another try?

Just as I'm warming up to the idea, her fingers trail down my chest, lingering on my zipper. Clearly, we're on the same page here.

But when my cock bobs in my jeans, urging me to take things further, it's like the blood stops pumping in my veins. A familiar and unwelcome zing of panic pulses through me, and I stumble back, breaking away from her touch.

Penelope's eyes widen and she gasps with surprise. "What is it? Did I do something wrong?"

"No, it's not you. It's . . ." I cut myself off mid-sentence. Was I really about to cite the oldest fucking line in the book? *It's not you; it's me.* This girl doesn't need my clichés, not even if they're true.

"Look, I'm sorry, I just . . ." I shove a hand through my hair, staring unseeing at the kitchen floor. I should say something. I owe it to her to say something. But the alarm bells going off in my head won't even let me form a coherent sentence, so I keep my mouth shut.

"You just what?"

Her tone is patient, not at all demanding, but I still feel put on the spot. When I finally have the balls to look at Penelope, her usual clear blue eyes are clouded with pain. Pain that I caused.

"Nothing. It's fine," I manage to say on a slow exhale.

Shit, I'm not even convincing myself.

Penelope's full lips part on a shaky sigh, her eyes desperately searching mine for the explanation that I'm not ready to give.

"Wolfie . . . you can tell me." She takes one hesitant step toward me, and I flinch back, keeping my distance. "Remember at the lake house? You told me so much, but if there's something else . . ."

Slowly, she reaches for my arm, but I pull away again, out of her reach.

I can't do this. Not now. Not with her.

"I have to go." The words cut through the air, clean and sharp. Final.

I turn, avoiding eye contact as I hurry toward the door, then shove my arms into the sleeves of my coat as I step into my boots, not even bothering to lace them up. I don't have the time. I need to get out of here.

"Wolfie, please." Penelope pleads, following a few steps behind me. "Please stay. We don't have to do *that*. You can talk to me."

Her words hit me like a sucker punch to the gut, but I don't so much as turn around to acknowledge them. Instead, I pull open the door and hurry down the stairs, stepping back into the biting early winter air.

The wind stings my cheeks, but I can't help but feel like I deserve it, both for letting things get so far with her and for bailing with no explanation. I don't know which is worse, but I do know that if I stuck around and took things further, I'd just be setting her up for even more pain. She's better off with me gone.

I hop on the train and ride it past my usual stop, all the way down to my favorite stretch of bars. Nothing sounds better right now than being one of hundreds of faceless, drunken strangers in a crowd. Plus, whiskey tastes better when someone else pours it for you, and I sure as hell need a drink.

My go-to spot is more packed than it should be on a weeknight, but I slip the bouncer a twenty, and in seconds I'm inside. Money talks, and I've got a few more bills in my wallet that are calling out for a Jameson neat.

Shouldering through the crowd, I make my way to the bar and manage to claim a free bar stool. I'll take it as a sign that I'm supposed to be here, drinking my problems away with some shitty club soundtrack in the background. If only I could find whoever's pouring the drinks down here.

My gaze travels down the bar and over a dozen unfamiliar faces, each of them laughing and sipping something strong. Eventually, I find my target, a guy dressed in head-to-toe black, taking an order from a dark-haired girl in a red dress.

Wait a second. I know that girl.

Suddenly, my mouth feels like the fucking Sahara Desert.

It's Tessa. I haven't spoken to her since I shut her down via text during Penelope's work retreat. Apparently, I'm staring a little too long, because her gaze meets mine and recognition flashes.

Shit. I could have looked away and played dumb, but it's too late now.

She mutters something to the bartender that I can't hear from this distance. Moments later, she's sauntering my way with a glass of Jameson and the kind of smug smile that irritates the hell out of me.

"Long time, no see." She slides the glass across the bar and straight into my palm.

Lord knows she's the last person I want to see right now, but I'm not turning down free booze, even if it is compliments of an old hookup.

"Hey, Tessa," I choke out. My grip on the glass tightens, and I knock back half of it in one swallow, letting the familiar punch of heat hit my stomach. It feels good in the worst way.

"You haven't been out lately." She props her elbows on the bar in a way that's clearly intended to showcase her tits.

"I've been busy."

"Too busy for me?" She bats her thick black lashes at me, jutting out her lower lip in a pout.

I'm not dignifying that with a response. As I stare into my whiskey, she wiggles in closer until we're inches apart, close enough that I can smell the whiskey on her breath.

"Listen, Wolf. Let's cut to the chase and get out of here." She trails her fingers from my shoulder to my bicep. "To your place?"

I can't shake her hand off me fast enough. "We're not doing that anymore, Tess." I look up from my glass in time to watch her lips pull into a tight frown.

"Why not? We had fun, didn't we? Why not have fun again?"

She squeezes my thigh under the bar. I have no choice but to physically lift her hand from my leg and move it away.

"I said no, Tess." My tone is firmer this time.

She scoffs and rolls her eyes at me. Luckily, she doesn't have a drink in her hand, or she might have thrown it in my face. But before she walks across the bar to flirt with the next unlucky bastard, she can't help but get in the last word.

"There's something wrong with you."

Her words sink into me like teeth. She's right. But she doesn't know the half of it.

Gulping down what's left in my glass, I flag down the bartender and get myself another Jameson, this time on the rocks. I need to slow myself down somehow, and the ice should keep me from tossing the whole thing back. But no amount of drinking could make me forget Tessa's words.

There's something wrong with you.

I've always known that to be true, but it hurts a whole lot more hearing someone else say it out loud. Even if it is an old hookup whose opinion shouldn't matter much.

It hasn't always been this way, though. Once upon a time, I was a normal horny teenager eager to experience sex and pleasure. But then one night when I was sixteen, I broke.

My dad's girlfriend came into my bedroom in the middle of the night, and I woke up to a hand that wasn't mine gripping me inside my boxers. It was foreign and strange, mostly because no one had ever touched me before. What made it even more so was she was someone that I'd looked at like a mother figure in my life.

At first, I was so stunned, I just lay there. My body wouldn't cooperate.

I wanted to shout at her to get out, but my voice wouldn't come. I wanted to push her hands away, but instead, I lay there motionless, unable to move an inch. I wanted her to know that my body's condition wasn't in response to her touch. I'd often woke up hard and aching, and now my body was betraying me.

Finally, I moved, rolling over to face the wall,

and she quietly left. But the damage was done. Something clicked off inside me after that.

It shattered all trust. It torpedoed everything. The next day, I thought I was doing the right thing by telling my dad. He brushed it off, said I probably just dreamed the whole thing and Janine would never do something like that. My dad not listening to me was nothing new, I'd spent most of my childhood ignored and neglected, but his rejection about this hurt worse than anything. After, I sunk into a deep depression. I was incapable of feeling pleasure. And even now, it still haunts me. That sickening creepy feeling that churns low in my stomach when I think about that night. That apathetic dread that slammed through me at my own dad's denial. It broke something inside me.

And more than that, it complicated my sex life. Before, I'd been a normal, horny teenager eager to experience sex and pleasure. But something had clicked off inside me after that. When I finally got around to losing my virginity, it was a quick, emotionless affair and that was still the way I preferred things. Quick. Efficient. With no room for feelings or emotion. Get in. Get off. Get out. There wasn't cuddling or comfort or kissing.

The old me was long gone, replaced with someone I hardly liked. Someone distant. The kind of guy who can manage to spend one night tangled up with the most beautiful girl he's ever laid eyes on, and be totally unable to let her touch him less than a week later.

If it were you, you'd probably be drinking alone on a weeknight too.

But the hurt in Penelope's eyes when I left tonight . . . *Fuck*, that destroyed me.

Penelope.

Just thinking her name makes my heart ache, and my body hum to life in new and strange ways.

She's different. I can see it in her expression and the hope that fills her wide blue eyes when she looks at me.

She thinks I'm a good man, a kind man, that I'd be a loving boyfriend who enjoys romantic movies and stolen kisses. The kind of man you could bring home to meet your parents, who would shake your dad's hand and say, *you've raised a hell of a daughter, sir*. And then everyone would have a good laugh.

But I'm none of those things. To be honest, I'm barely functioning most days. I work, sleep, and hit the gym, filling my time so I don't have to sit around and think about why I'm so broken. And when the ache inside me becomes too much to bear, I get drunk and fumble my way through a quick fuck that only leaves me feeling worse. Guilty and confused.

Lather. Rinse. Repeat.

I've been this way my entire adult life. And now Penelope with her pretty mouth and her shining optimism wants me to change? To smile at her and pull her into my arms and hold her while we make love?

It just doesn't work that way.

Soon enough she'd discover what a piece of shit I am, all about my fucked-up past and why I couldn't even keep Tessa happy. Then Penelope would leave too, and I'd be alone again, which is exactly the way it's supposed to be.

Twelve

PENELOPE

"**S**o he just . . . left?" Scarlett blinks at me in disbelief from behind her coffee mug, her mouth hanging open in shock.

We've spent the better portion of our lunch breaks huddled in this West Loop coffee shop, hashing out the details of the last few weeks of my dramatic life. It's quite the story, beginning with Wolfie playing the role of my fake boyfriend on a work retreat, and ending with him walking out on me last night. A story that, unfortunately, ends with a bunch of big, bold question marks instead of a happy ending.

I nod somberly. "Yup. He just broke away from me while we were kissing and bolted out the door."

Scarlett's eyes are brimming with such intense sympathy, I can't even look at her without feeling pathetic. Instead, I focus on stirring my spoon in lazy circles through my hot chocolate.

Well, it's really more like room-temperature chocolate now with how long I've been rambling. Normally, I'm a latte girl, but when a man flees your apartment in the middle of a hot make-out session, you buy yourself a damn hot cocoa. Tack on the homemade marshmallows this place advertises, and I couldn't say no.

"Okay, so then what?" She splays her fingers across the white faux-marble table, leaning in with anticipation. "Did he come back? Did he call you and explain himself, begging for forgiveness?"

Girl, I wish.

I release a slow breath and shake my head. "Nope. That's it. He just left, and I haven't heard from him since."

The truth is, I wasn't sure if I should text him, or call, or just wait for him to make contact when he's ready. It's like he's got the weight of the world on his shoulders. While he's told me a little about his preferences, he hasn't told me the reasons *why* he is the way he is. And I honestly just don't understand him as much as I'd like to.

Scarlett nods slowly, her brow furrowing as she digests my words. "Okay, so . . . that's *a lot*."

"Yeah. Tell me about it."

For a moment, the only sound between us is Scarlett's manicured fingers drumming on the side of her white ceramic mug. "And you're sure things were going well before that? He wasn't giving off any weird vibes?"

Talk about a loaded question. Wolfie Cox is in a constant state of giving off weird vibes. But Scarlett knows this—we've all hung out in the same circle of friends for years.

Actually, Scarlett's known Wolfie longer than I have. I only met him through my brother once they became roommates. Scarlett and Caleb have been inseparable for years before that. She's always been a bit of an older-sister type to me, which actually gives me an idea. I should ask for her advice on all this. Plus, she is a few years older than me . . . and she's been through her share of awful guys. I'm sure she has some wisdom.

But as I open my mouth to speak, I realize that would involve me telling her about Wolfie's intimacy issues, and exposing his insecurities doesn't feel like the right move. He told me those things in confidence, and even if I have no idea where I stand with the man, I'm not going to betray his trust.

Maybe this is just part of who he is. Maybe he

runs when he gets scared . . . or overwhelmed. Or turned on? *God, I don't know.* I heave out a sigh and press my fingers into my temples.

Things started off so easy last night. It didn't seem like he was worried about anything. He was sweet and easygoing, his usual armor of anxiety nowhere to be found. It was like I'd had him over for dinner dozens of times. The conversation was easy and natural. Even when things got physical, he was still so relaxed. Until, well, until he suddenly wasn't.

"I swear it was smooth sailing up until then. Totally normal. And then out of the blue, he grabs his coat and runs." My stomach hollows out at the memory, the sting of rejection as Wolfie's gray eyes went dull just before he dashed out my door.

Retelling the story is proving to be as hurtful and confusing as living it out in real time. With the edge of my spoon, I scoop a gooey melted marshmallow from my mug and pop it between my lips, letting the sweet, sticky sugar rush go straight to my head. They say laughter is the best medicine, but I'd have to argue that sugar gives it a run for its money.

She nods once. "Wolfie is a complicated guy. He deserves the world, but try telling him that."

I make a sound of agreement, thoughtfully eating a second marshmallow.

Scarlett pushes back from the table a little, as if to give herself space to process this mess. "Well, I can confidently say that when you told me we needed to discuss your boy problems, I definitely wasn't expecting *that*."

I lift a shoulder, a hint of a sad smile pulling at my lips. "What can I say? I'm always full of surprises."

She only shrugs.

Not that my attraction to Wolfie should come as much of a surprise to her. The only person who knows as much about my Wolfie fantasies as my journal is Scarlett. And thank God she does, because I can't hold all this in without inevitably exploding, and I certainly can't tell the rest of our friends. Scarlett is so perceptive, she guessed at my feelings one night over cocktails, and I've been confiding in her ever since.

Scarlett chews her lower lip in thought for a long moment, then straightens in her seat, her eyes brightening with realization. "Here's a thought. What if dinner didn't sit right with him, and he had to . . . you know." She clutches her stomach, miming illness, which earns her a much-deserved scowl from me.

"This was not an invitation to make fun of my cooking, Scar. I'm looking for actual advice."

She folds her arms over her chest and shrugs. "I'm just saying, rosé and alfredo sauce don't exactly mix. Maybe he wasn't feeling well."

Deflated, I sink deeper into my chair. Part of me wants to believe she's right. It would be less painful than the alternative explanation—that Wolfie just isn't interested in being physical with me again.

I must be staring into my hot cocoa for a little too long, though, because moments later, I feel the reassuring warmth of Scarlett's hand over mine.

"I'm just kidding, P. Don't overthink it. You know how weird Wolfie can be. But you said he opened up to you at the lake house, right? That's a big deal. Especially for him." When I don't respond, she gives my hand a gentle squeeze. "Hey, I bet you learned more about him in one night than the rest of us have over the last four years."

"You're right," I say begrudgingly, softly squeezing her hand back. "He was just so vulnerable that night. So open and honest. I want to see that side of him all the time, you know?"

"I get it. And you deserve that," she says firmly. "But maybe he's not ready yet. Don't force it. Just be your usual supportive self, and it will come."

A low groan rolls from me as I bury my face in my hands. "Ugh, you're right, you're right." I split my fingers enough to peer out at her. "Why do you always have to be right?"

Her laugh is soft and bubbly as she tosses her auburn hair over one shoulder. "I can't help it. Being right is in my DNA. But so is being on time, and I do have a meeting with a potential client in ten."

"Oh, don't let me keep you." I press to my feet, shooing her toward the door. "Get out of here. I'll have plenty of drama to talk through another day."

She cocks her head, barely holding back a smile. "You sure? I don't want to pull a Wolfie and bolt right in the middle of something."

My eyes narrow in disapproval, but I can't help the smile pulling at my lips. "If this mug weren't ceramic, I'd throw it at you, you know that?"

A mischievous grin breaks out on her face as she shoots me a wink. "I know. But it is, and you won't. Let's do this again soon, though, okay? I like this place."

We return our empty mugs to the dirty dish bin and button up our coats, hurrying through our good-byes at the door so as to not keep Scarlett's client waiting.

She makes a sound that's some combination of a sympathy and a sigh, laying a hand on my shoulder like a proud mother. "You're a rock star, you know that? Wolfie's a lucky guy."

I smile, but there's a sadness behind it.

Here's to hoping he thinks so too.

Thirteen

WOLFIE

When Connor walks through the door of our storefront on Wednesday morning, I hardly recognize the man.

First of all, he's forty minutes late, which is entirely out of character. Tardiness has never been Connor's style—first, because he rides his motorcycle everywhere, meaning that he can weave through all the traffic on Lake Shore Drive and handily beat any of us to work, bars, anywhere we're meeting up.

Second, the guy looks like a ghost, and it's not just the pale, haunted look on his face. His hair is a mess, and I'd put money down that he didn't shave today, his overgrown stubble creeping down the front of his throat. No way am I letting this bastard wander into neck-beard territory. Somebody needs an intervention.

"Did somebody just dig you out of your grave?"

Connor doesn't even respond, which is all the proof I need that something's up. If he were in his right mind, no way would he let me get away with a comment like that.

But instead of hitting me with one of his usual digs, he just plods through the store, dragging his feet along the black tile. When he finally joins us behind the counter, he leans against the back wall with a defeated huff. If I didn't know better, I'd think he needed the support of the wall to stay upright.

I look toward Ever, then Hayes, hoping one of them has an explanation for Connor's behavior, but no dice. Hayes shrugs, and Ever just shakes his head.

Great. I guess I'll be the one doing the detective work this morning. As if I didn't already have enough on my plate.

When I turn back toward Connor, he's staring down at the floor, totally zoned out. "Hello? You there, Blake?"

I wave a hand in front of Connor's face, and he startles out of his daze, blinking at me with the kind of confused look he normally reserves for math or girls who turn him down.

"What? Uh, yeah. I'm fine," he grumbles, one hand rubbing the tension from the back of his neck. "Totally fine."

He's obviously *not* fine. How am I not supposed to be worried about him when he's acting completely deranged?

I side-eye the hell out of him. Connor's easygoing charm is nowhere to be found, and it's more unnerving than I expected it to be. He's always been the glue that holds our crew together.

The last few years of starting a business together hasn't always been easy, and there have been times when tempers flared and testosterone-fueled arguments broke out. Connor's good-natured reliability always got us through. He was the one to step in, putting himself in the middle of any disagreement. He's the person you can count on one hundred percent of the time to be calm and collected. Levelheaded. Chill.

But right now, that guy is gone. And in his place is a man I don't recognize. It rocks me to my core.

But before we can get any deeper into it, the bell on the door chimes, and in walks a customer. A middle-aged woman with a brunette bob, her winter coat zipped up to her neck. She gives the four of us a quick smile before shuffling back toward the couples' corner. It seems like she knows what she's looking for, and thank fuck for that, because Connor is the one who usually makes the sales pitches around here.

I reach for our speaker system and dial up the volume on the ambient music. Just two notches, enough to hopefully drown out this conversation.

"Hey. What's going on with you?" I shoot Connor one of my *no bullshit* looks. I'm not messing around here. There's something up with him, and we're not going to make it through a full workday if our top salesman is as useless as a one-legged cat.

Connor stuffs his hands into his pockets, barely managing half a shrug. "Nothing much. What's up with you?"

Fucking hell. I don't have the patience for this today.

I sigh, folding my arms over my chest. "No, I mean what's *going on* with you? You look like shit."

He scoffs. "Thanks, jackass. You don't look so hot yourself."

"No, I mean you look like a zombie with a third-degree hangover." I raise one eyebrow at him for emphasis.

I should know. I'm nursing a mild hangover myself. I may have gotten a third glass of Jameson last night after Tessa told me off.

Between proving to both Penelope and myself that I'm too much of a mess for her and swerving my ex-hookup at the bar, there was a lot of edge to take off.

And to be honest, I'm still reeling. Not so much from Tessa, but from Penelope. I hurt her, and that's bothering me. But I'm not going to let that show. And that's more than Connor can say about whatever's eating him up inside.

"I'm fine, okay?"

His voice is louder this time, strident enough to get the attention of our newest customer. She snaps her head toward the register, frowns at Connor, then goes back to reading the ingredients on the lavender massage oil in her hand.

Gripping Connor by the elbow, I pull him into the back office and bark at Hayes to man the register, tugging the door shut behind me. Connor flashes me an uncertain look but it's too late. I have him cornered.

"C'mon, dude." He groans, trying to maneuver past me, but I counter, anticipating his every move. When he steps left, I step right, blocking him with squared shoulders and a tight frown.

"I'm not letting you leave unless you agree to go back home and straight to bed."

He levels me with a glare. "I don't need to go home," he forces out through gritted teeth, but his stern look quickly fades away to worry. "I, uh, actually . . . if I'm going anywhere, I need to go to the car dealership."

I flinch back an inch. The car dealership? Is this the same Connor who once told me he'd sooner lick the floor of the train station than pay for a vehicle sticker just for the privilege to park in the city?

"The dealership? What, does your motorcycle need work?"

He swallows hard, slowly shaking his head. "Nope. Sold it."

All right, now I'm positive he's sick in the head. No fucking way did Connor Blake sell his baby. He cares more about that thing than any woman he's brought back to our apartment in the last year and a half.

I squint at him, assessing him for signs of sarcasm, but I come up empty. All I can do is call his bluff. "You're lying."

"Why would I lie about that?" He frowns, his eyes brimming with something close to . . . sadness? Like he's grieving a loss. And in many ways, he is, if what he says is true. That bike was like his trophy wife.

"So, why'd you sell it?" I press, but the second I ask, his guard instantly shoots back up.

"None of your business."

"Of course it's my business." I huff, taking a step closer. "My roommate just sold his most prized possession and is buying a car, which he said he'd never do. You're not telling me something."

"Can you just drop it?" His voice is strained, but I have no intention of letting this go.

"Absolutely not."

He sighs behind a clenched jaw, his hands balling into fists. "And why not?"

I nearly laugh. Do I really have to spell it out for him? "Because it's fucking annoying to look at you, know something's up, and not have you tell me what it is."

No sooner are the words out of my mouth than

the realization of their weight hits me. Like someone just swung a pillowcase full of bricks directly at my head.

Someone you care about not telling you what's wrong with them.

Well, *shit*, that sounds familiar. It's exactly what I'm doing to Penelope. I haven't opened up to her and told her about my issues, but now I'm pissed because Connor is doing the same thing to me.

Connor looks me over with suspicion. "Now you're the one who looks like a hungover zombie," he says with a vicious smirk. "What gives?"

I let go of a shaky breath. I feel like the biggest hypocrite in the city of Chicago, and not telling him what's going on just solidifies that title. But I'm not about to go there with Connor. He'd break my neck if he knew any of what's gone down between me and his sister.

"Make you a deal," I say. "I don't make you fess up to whatever your problem is, and I don't have to tell you shit about mine."

His chin dips in a firm nod. "Sold."

It's quiet between us, and for a second I think we're going to shake on it or something. But then

Connor clears his throat into his fist, shifting his weight between his feet.

"I, uh . . . I'm serious about the car dealership, though. Any chance I can hitch a ride?"

I snatch my keys from my back pocket and tip my head toward the back door. "We'll let Hayes and Ever man the fort. Let's roll."

We drive in near complete silence, just the sound of the radio and the occasional direction from Connor. But silence doesn't bother me. It never has.

Plus, my mind is busy working through other things, like how I'm going to make things right with Penelope. That is, if she'll even forgive me for ghosting her the other night after she made me a home-cooked meal. Lord knows it'll take a long-ass time for me to even forgive myself. But if there's anyone worth being vulnerable with, it's her.

"This is the one." Connor points me toward the parking lot of the car dealership ahead with its bright lights and row after row of shiny new cars. "The one with the SUVs."

I have to swallow my laugh. Connor Blake driving an SUV? I must be living in an alternate reality.

And in this reality, maybe I can show Penelope that I can let my guard down. All the way down.

Fourteen

WOLFIE

hen Connor announces his sister is coming over tonight, it's unexpected. And when Penelope shows up later with a six-pack of his favorite beer and a smile on her face, it's hard to pretend I'm not affected.

Things have been a little confusing between us lately, but there's one thing that's crystal clear—we have a strong mutual attraction. Because I'd have to be blind not to notice the way her eyes keep straying over to mine, or the way her hand lingered when she passed me a beer earlier—like she wanted to keep touching me, however brief it might be.

Connor seems oblivious, thank fucking God.

It was a long week of work, and I'm thankful for the chance to blow off a little steam. And the view doesn't suck, if I'm being honest. The sight of Penelope sitting on the couch across from me, dressed in a pair of skintight jeans and a pink sweater that hugs her perfect tits? Yeah, sign me the heck up.

"So, what's new, baby sister?" Connor asks, settling into the armchair beside the couch with his ankle crossed over one knee.

He's been so distracted lately, but right now, about four beers in, he seems relaxed. I wonder if Penelope noticed that he's been off too.

Wonder if that's part of why she came over tonight . . . maybe she's here to cheer him up? I can't let myself believe she's actually here to see me. That could mess with a guy's head pretty good. Especially when I've been nothing but confusing with her.

"Just living the dream," she answers with a smile.

I chuckle and listen in rapt attention as she fills us in on work and the latest with that douche Spencer. Connor and I both laugh at her impression of him trying to fix the copier.

The conversation flows easily for a while, but we don't talk about the elephant in the room— Connor selling his prized motorcycle. Then again, maybe Penelope doesn't know yet. The guy is clearly keeping a few secrets, and I'm not going to be the one to out him. It would be more than a bit hypocritical.

When Penelope excuses herself to go to the kitchen for another beer, it takes every bit of will-power I have not to follow her into the kitchen for some privacy. We still haven't gotten the chance to talk after I just dashed out of her place the other night when things got hot and heavy—but it doesn't seem like Penelope is going to hold a grudge.

What's that called when someone lets you off the hook, even when you really don't deserve it? Oh yeah, *grace*.

Penelope is giving me grace. She hasn't demanded answers or questioned me. It just shows what a truly amazing woman she is. She's mature and responsible and kind. And she sure as shit doesn't deserve to end up with a guy like me, but for right now, I'm counting myself lucky just to be in her presence. Just the chance to sit here and listen to her talk and see her pretty blue eyes light up when she looks at me is enough.

"Should we call it a night?" Connor asks, stretching his arms across the back of the couch. "You're obviously staying the night," he says to Penelope.

To my surprise, she doesn't protest. "That works."

I'm relieved when she agrees to sleep on the couch, because I wouldn't want her taking a cab at this time of night.

Connor and Penelope head off in search of extra blankets and pillows. Since it would probably look strange if I lingered—I'm not here to tuck Penelope in, for fuck's sake—I head to my room, calling out a good-night to them both on my way.

But I'm not tired, and it takes me a long time to relax once I do lie down.

About twenty minutes later, my bedroom door opens. Then the corner of my mattress dips, and I open my eyes to see Penelope crawling across the mattress toward me in the darkness.

A surprised sound leaves my lips as her mouth presses to mine.

"Penelope?" I say warily.

She makes a shushing sound and crawls on top of me. My heart takes off in a gallop. I can't think straight with her straddling me.

"What are you doing?"

"Seducing you," she murmurs, her voice husky. "Is it working?"

We've both been drinking. This isn't the way I wanted things to go for us. Especially not with her brother nearby.

"Connor will hear you," I whisper.

She shakes her head. "Not if we're quiet."

Then she leans in for a kiss, and I'm powerless to refuse her. *Bad idea, Wolfie*, my brain warns.

Her mouth moves enthusiastically over mine, and I kiss her back as emotions war inside me. But she feels so good with her warm curves on top of me, and the scent of her shampoo filling my senses. My hands wander to her ass and I tug her even closer, lifting my hips so I can press my quickly hardening cock against her.

All the breath rushes out of my lungs at once. I feel almost light-headed. Hot. Aroused. And stressed the fuck out because there's no way this can go any further.

"Penelope, we can't."

Her mouth leaves my neck, and she gives me a look. "Because you don't want to?"

"Because your brother is on the other side of this wall."

She moves off of me, sliding to the bed beside me. "You're lying. You just don't want me."

I hate that she thinks that. But what else is she supposed to think? I keep pushing her away. I curl my fingers around my erection through my boxer briefs. "Does this look like I don't want you?"

Her eyes widen. "*Oh*."

"I would pound you against the bed right now if I could."

"You can." She's breathless when she responds, then whispers, "Yes. To the pounding."

I chuckle darkly. "Not like this. Not when we're drunk and hiding from Connor."

Disappointment flashes over her features. And then she's leaning over, kissing my neck, sucking feverish little spots all over the column of my throat.

A hot zing of arousal flashes through my veins, making my groin tighten and my dick swell in eager anticipation. *God*, I want her. I've never wanted anything more.

Her voice soft and needy, she says, "Tell me what you'd do to me if you could . . ."

I touch her cheek, bringing her lips up to mine

once again for a kiss. She whimpers lightly when my tongue touches hers.

It takes a heroic amount of strength on my part when I pull back, breaking our kiss. "You really want to know?"

After a beat of silence, she gives me an eager look, pressing her lips together as she nods her head.

"First, I'd strip you naked," I whisper, pressing a kiss to her mouth. "Then I'd suck on those pretty little nipples, lick and tug on them with hot, wet suction until you were squirming."

She makes that needy whimpering sound again, and it sends a holt of heat straight to my balls. *Damn.*

"Then I'd touch your pussy, rub your clit softly, just to tease . . . just to make sure you were wet for me." My voice is a husky rasp, barely above a whisper, but Penelope's eyes are glued to mine. I wish like anything my hand really was in her panties right now, rubbing slow circles that made her eyes sink closed.

"What else?" she murmurs.

I press a kiss to her neck. "I'd play with your pussy for a while. Make sure you were soaking wet for me . . . about to come . . . just from me rubbing your clit." Her lips part and she draws in a quick breath. "Then I'd sink my cock inside your perfect, tight pussy and start pounding hard . . . I wouldn't hold back, sweetheart. You'd have to take all of me."

"I could take all of you," she whispers, her voice ragged.

I tilt my head, giving her a hard look. "But could you keep quiet for me? While my thick cock is filling you?"

She licks her lips but doesn't answer.

"I can go for a long time," I remind her.

She nods once, meeting my eyes, likely remembering what I'd told her before . . . that it takes me a long time to come. Although, right now I doubt that would be true. If she so much as wrapped me in her fist and gave my cock a few tugs, I'd embarrass myself and jizz all over her hand.

"I'd take it all," she says softly, encouragingly, her eyes pleading with mine.

"That's good. Because I'd want to fill you, claim that pussy. And I'd keep hammering it until you came all over my dick."

She whimpers again, and the sound rips through

me. The mental image jumps into my head of her on her knees, taking my cock into her mouth, licking and sucking off all of her sweet cream. I force in a sharp inhale and try to cool myself down.

I didn't even know this side of myself existed. This dirty-talking, sex-forward fuckboy. But Penelope seems into it. And everything I've said is true. I do want her right now. I'd fuck her hard and fast . . . or slow and deep . . . whichever she wanted.

I'm *this close* to grabbing her and just saying *fuck it*. Who cares if Connor's bed is on the other side of this wall?

Thankfully, cooler thoughts prevail.

We can't. Not like this.

With one final kiss to her lips, I take her hand and tug her from the bed. I adjust my cock inside my boxer briefs, since walking is a little difficult at the moment, and escort her to the door. "But none of that can happen tonight."

She's glassy-eyed, flushed with arousal, but she nods. "You suck."

"Good things come to those who wait." I press one last kiss to her forehead.

"Good night, Wolfie."

"Night, sweetheart."

When I open the door, she tiptoes from my room and back down the hall into the darkened living room.

I stand there at the door, even after she's gone, and squeeze my eyes closed.

When I crawl back into my bed, I can still smell her shampoo on my pillow. I close my eyes and inhale as my right hand slips under the elastic of my boxer briefs. I'm as hard as a fucking fence post, and as I run my hand up and down my cock, I draw a shaky breath as pleasure washes over me.

I wonder if Penelope is doing the same thing on the couch. Maybe she's rubbing her clit like I wanted to . . . or maybe she's sinking her fingers into her warmth beneath the blankets. The thought only makes me harder. My fist moves in short, efficient strokes, and I clench my jaw as blinding pleasure riots through every cell in my body. It's not long before I come all over my stomach.

Fuck.

I'm breathing hard and my heart is beating out of control when I grab a wad of tissues to clean myself up with.

I have no idea what the hell just happened, but

it's time to face reality. This isn't just about sex anymore. Things between Penelope and me are evolving. I find myself opening up to her in ways I haven't with anyone else before. Wanting things I've never wanted before.

It's a dangerous situation to be in—with my roommate's sister, of all people. But it doesn't scare me nearly as much as it used to.

Fifteen

WOLFIE

After trudging up the steps, I enter a small office. The receptionist asks my name and then waves me on through the door at the far end of the room.

"Go on in. She's expecting you."

With nervous knots tying intricate patterns inside my stomach, I step through the doorway, but stop almost immediately.

A middle-aged woman sits behind a desk. Her hair is dark but threaded with silver, and she smiles and removes a pair of purple reading glasses when she spots me.

"Hi there. Come on in."

I take one more tentative step forward, then stop.

This was a stupid idea. My life has felt a little out of control lately. I thought talking with someone—a professional—might help. Now I don't think I can go through with it.

"I'm sorry for wasting your time. I don't know why I'm here."

"It's fine. Wolfgang, right?"

"Wolfie." I nod.

"Wolfie, it's fine. You're not wasting my time. And it's okay to feel apprehension. But since you're here, maybe we can talk for a few minutes. Please sit down." She gestures toward the seating in the office. When I don't budge, the therapist raises her hands in a show of surrender, her palms facing me. "Whatever you want to do. I'm only here to help."

I release a slow breath. "I guess I could stay for a few minutes."

She gives me a warm smile, but I can feel her eyes appraising me, watching everything as I select a seat—the chair across from her desk, rather than one of the cozy armchairs under the windows.

"So, how does this work?" I ask, pressing my hands into my knees.

God, I feel so jumpy, so on edge. This is ridiculous. It's just that I've never opened up and told someone my truth before. But now . . . with Penelope . . . it's different. She has me wanting to try things I've never been interested in before. Intimacy. A relationship, maybe. Hell, I don't know.

"Well, usually people start off by telling me what's going on in their lives. Usually, they're here because they need help navigating a situation or working through a season they're facing."

I nod. "Makes sense."

Removing her glasses, she smiles again, lines forming beside her eyes as she watches me. She seems nice enough. I guess I just didn't count on it being so hard to open up to a complete stranger, even if this is her job.

"So, what's been going on in your life, Wolfie?"

I press my hands together in my lap. "Well, um . . . my roommate's being really secretive lately."

She doesn't say anything else. She just keeps watching me, and when she finally opens her mouth to reply, the words are not at all what I'm expecting. "I don't think you're here to talk about your roommate."

"You don't?"

She shakes her head.

I release a long, strained exhale. *Why the fuck am I here?*

The other night, when Penelope sneaked into my room, I found myself wanting to be someone different, to be bold and reckless and just give in to everything. But sadly for me, when I woke up in the morning, I was still that same broken guy. I have no idea why, but I thought this would help. Now it feels way too invasive.

"I'm sorry. I'm just not comfortable with this."

The therapist gives me a sympathetic look. "I'm sorry for pushing. Why don't you tell me what's been going on with your *roommate*?"

A wary smile crosses my lips. The way she said the word *roommate* implied she's giving me permission to talk about myself, but under the guise of these being someone else's problems. But hey, it's enough for me.

So I do want any coward would do. I tell her all about "my roommate's" problems.

His life-long struggle with intimacy. His past of no-strings-attached encounters with women. And finally, him meeting this great girl who makes him imagine things he's never imagined with anyone else, and the fears that come along with that.

When I'm done, I listen to every fucking piece of advice she lays out.

I have no idea if any of it will help, but it's a start. And when I leave forty minutes later, I feel ten pounds lighter.

Sixteen

PENELOPE

On a Friday night in Chicago, my neighborhood is the place to be.

It's part of the reason I chose an apartment in this area, just above the chaos of downtown while still being nice and close to the lake. With all the trendy bars, cozy coffee shops, and some of the best restaurants on the north side, I live right in the epicenter of every twenty-something's weekend plans.

Even November's plummeting temperatures can't keep away the swarms of people filtering in and out of bars for happy hour, toasting to the end of a long workweek. And on any other weekend, I'm usually among that crowd, a strong drink in one hand and a half-priced appetizer in the other. But tonight, none of that is on the agenda.

Actually, I have no idea what *is* on the agenda. What I do know is that when Wolfie texted me saying he had something to show me, I didn't ask many questions for fear of scaring him off again. More than anything, I was relieved to hear from him at all, based on how we left things last week.

Now I'm riding shotgun in his car, admiring Wolfie's seasoned city driving as he expertly weaves us through the traffic that Friday nights in Chicago are so famous for. Rush hour in the city always turns me into a white-knuckled stress bomb, but my chauffeur for the evening is seemingly unaffected by the chaos. It's a nice change of pace.

"This is insane," I mutter, motioning toward the shit show that we're bearing witness to.

When a nearby driver lays on his horn, I jump at least three inches out of my seat. Meanwhile, Wolfie seems totally unfazed.

"Tell me your secrets," I say. "How did you become such an expert in city driving?"

"Practice," he says matter-of-factly. "I grew up here. But the roads won't be so bad where we're going."

I pause, wary of pressing my luck with questions, but ultimately ask in a small voice, "And, um, where is that exactly?"

Wolfie takes his eyes off the road for a second, just long enough to offer me the slightest hint of a smile. "You'll see."

As we head west, away from the lake and past the more developed parts of the city, both the drinking crowds and the traffic dissipate. Whatever it is that he wants me to see, it sure is awfully far from either of our homes.

A full thirty minutes pass and we're still driving, making our way farther and farther away from any part of the city that's familiar to me. Soon, the streets we're traveling are lined with more old-school corner stores than trendy cocktail bars, and the sidewalks are roadside are a bit more cluttered with litter, shattered liquor bottles and plastic bags.

I've ridden the bus through this part of the city before, but I've never gotten off here. Never had a reason to. It's the kind of place you pass through without stopping, the city equivalent to a flyover state. It's not dangerous, per se, but it's not the kind of place where a girl should be wandering around alone.

Luckily, I'm not alone. I'm with Wolfie, who looks apathetic as usual as he turns away from the string of abandoned storefronts and down a more residential road.

"Did we make a wrong turn somewhere?" My teeth sink into my lower lip as I size up the run-down apartment buildings lining the block, each of them shedding shingles and siding like old skin.

Wolfie shakes his head, steering us straight ahead. "Nope. Almost there."

I shift in my seat, trying not to seem unsettled by our surroundings. Both the neighborhood and the anticipation have me feeling fidgety. I'm the type who likes to have a plan, the type who needs to know what to expect.

Two blocks later, he parks on the street between an old truck and a minivan that's held together with the power of duct tape. I blink at Wolfie, waiting for the admission that he took a wrong turn after all and didn't want to fess up. Instead, he frees himself from his seat belt and hops out of the car.

All-righty then. I guess we're doing this.

Whatever *this* is.

Deep breaths, Pen. You can be spontaneous.

I join him on the sidewalk. To my surprise, his fingers lace through mine, sending a warm rush of adrenaline prickling through my veins.

The last time we were together, things got pretty heated. I can't help but reflect on Wolfie's behavior that night and the things he said. Maybe he was so free because he knew nothing could actually happen between us—not with my brother right next door. It's an interesting theory, anyway.

But right now, I don't have time to analyze it because our palms are pressed together tight enough for me to feel his heartbeat, and all the uncertainty between us washes away. For now, it's just him and me, hand in hand, and I would follow him anywhere.

We fall into step, strolling down the sidewalk for half a block until Wolfie halts in front of an old brick four-story building.

"This is it."

He stares up at the building, his eyes full of every emotion. Pride. Sadness. Love. Anger. His reaction is far more interesting than the building itself, with its boarded-up windows and unremarkable brick exterior.

I try to take it in, to see whatever he's seeing, but I come up blank. It's just an old run-down apartment building that looks like it's set to be demolished.

"What is this place?" I ask.

Wolfie swallows, his eyes still locked ahead.

"Something I wanted to show you."

It strikes me that this is Wolfie letting me in. I'm barely breathing, recognizing this is a big moment between us. "What is it?"

"This is where I grew up."

Suddenly, it feels like somebody planted a firecracker in my stomach. I knew Wolfie was a born-and-raised Chicagoan, but I've always figured he was from the suburbs or somewhere else on the outskirts of town. But this isn't suburbia. This is an urban hellscape. How has he never brought this up?

"It was me, my dad, and Maren," he says, pointing toward the top apartment on the left. "In that two-bedroom up there."

I glance up at the side of the building where he's indicating and squint, trying to picture him here. "You wanted to show me . . . where you grew up?"

He nods. "I know you've had a lot of questions."

I give him a small smile. "Your past is your business. And I'm happy to be patient. I just . . . want to understand you is all."

"I know," he says softly.

"What about your mom?" I ask on a whisper.

"She wasn't in the picture. It was just us and Dad. Well, and his revolving door of girlfriends. And there was one . . ." Wolfie's voice tightens, then trails off into a long, tense silence. "There was one who was especially bad," he finally says, like he's finishing a memory he would rather not face.

I draw in a slow, shaky breath, releasing it through my teeth.

What do I say? What questions are the right questions? Am I overstepping?

There's no way of quieting all the questions overlapping in my brain. All I can do is trust my gut and remember what Scarlett said. *Just be your usual supportive self, and the rest will come.*

God, I hope she's right.

It's only now that I realize Wolfie and I are still holding hands, and I give him a quick, reassuring squeeze, then drag my thumb along the expanse of his palm. "We don't have to talk about it if you don't want to."

"I do want to," he says firmly, his voice gruff and sure. "I want you to understand." His chest rises and falls in quick, measured breaths, his gaze still fixed on the front window of his old apartment.

His eyes are wild and worried, but I don't want him to be anxious. "It's okay," I say, tightening my hand around his. "You can tell me anything."

After a long, uneasy moment, he pushes back his shoulders and speaks, as emotionless as if he were reading from a phone book. "She came into my room one night. My dad's girlfriend. Her name was Janine. I was sixteen. It was late. The room was dark. But I felt her sit down on the edge of the bed. And then," he pauses, drawing another slow breath, "she touched me."

My heart lodges in my throat, and it feels like there's no oxygen left. I can't catch my breath. She touched him? His dad's girlfriend? This poor, broken man. I had no idea. He's been living with this pain all this time?

"I am so, so sorry, Wolfie," I whisper after a long, pain-filled silence. It's the only thing I can think to say. But no amount of apologies could ever be enough. Not for what he's been through. Once the initial shock wears off, a second thought rises to the surface. "Does your dad know?"

Wolfie nods somberly, his jaw clenched. "Told him the next morning. He brushed it off, said I probably just dreamed the whole thing and Janine would never do something like that. I thought I was doing the right thing by telling him, but I guess—"

"You *were* doing the right thing," I say quickly, interrupting. "I'm so sorry he didn't take you seriously."

"It was a long time ago. But it . . . you know. Complicated a couple things."

I bite my cheek, my head bobbing in a slow, sympathetic nod. "Of course it did. And that's not your fault." I mean every single one of those words.

My chest aches for him. For this truth he's been burdened with for so many years, not feeling comfortable to share this horror with anyone. How would he ever feel comfortable opening up if his own father didn't believe him? But Wolfie felt comfortable with me, and that makes my heart soar.

Maybe this step out of his comfort zone was to bring me understanding, or maybe it's part of him healing. I'm not sure, but I am grateful.

Realization shoots through me.

Wolfie has secrets that he doesn't want others to know. He has childhood pain and trauma. And as a result, sex can be difficult for him.

My throat is tight and my stomach is knotted. I wish I could fix this for him, but I know I can't on my own. It's his to endure. All I can do is be here, stand beside him, support him.

We stand wordlessly for a good long while, taking in the apartment building and all the old haunted memories that live there. When Wolfie finally breaks the silence, it's with a low chuckle of disbelief.

"I can't believe this place is still here. Thought they would've torn it down by now." His mouth curls into a small, sad smile, his hand gripping mine extra tight. "But I'm glad it's still here. So I could show you."

He turns to me, his bottomless gray eyes locking with mine. He doesn't have to say another word. Just the way he looks at me, like he's staring straight into my soul, says it all.

In a lot of ways, Wolfie is a lot like the building he grew up in. Worse for wear, but still standing strong despite everything it's endured.

"Thank you for telling me," I say in a small voice as the weight of his admission still rocks through me. "It means the world to me, and I will do whatever I can to help you. Whatever you need, Wolfie, please know that you can always count on me."

After a few more moments, we leave in silence. On the drive back to my apartment, it's like the fog of tension has lifted and Wolfie is a whole new man.

He points out the parks he went to growing up, the corner stores where he and Maren used to pool their money and buy bags of chips and packs of gum. For as broken as his childhood was, there were brighter memories too, little golden moments shining through the cracks in the concrete. And he's all too eager to share them with me.

By the time we pull up in front of my building, I feel closer to him than ever. Like his chipped edges all make sense. I want to keep driving with him, to learn this whole city through his eyes. I want to know every story and every scar. And it seems like he's finally brave enough to show me.

"Thanks for coming with me," Wolfie says as he shifts the car into park. "For letting me share that with you."

"You don't have to thank me," I say, correcting him. "I want to know that stuff. To learn everything about you."

And I realize my words are true. Things didn't start out this way between us, but they're changing. I want to be here for him, to help him work through his hang-ups. It's no trouble at all, despite what he thinks. It's a privilege to know that he trusts me with this stuff.

I reach over the console, taking Wolfie's hand in mine. He doesn't flinch away, just lets me trace the lifeline of his palm with light, reassuring strokes.

"Well, if you'd like to keep learning. You know. Stick around." He pauses, wrapping his fingers tight around my thumb and treats me to a gentle smile. "I think I'd really like that."

"Yeah? I think I'd really like that too."

I'm not quite sure who makes the first move. All I know is that moments later, we're sharing the sweetest, softest kiss I've ever known, each touch of his lips to mine more grateful than the last. There's something about the way this man kisses that's unlike anything I've ever experienced before. His earthy, masculine scent coupled with the tender strokes of his tongue against mine is the most perfect thing.

When I break away from our kiss, I trail my fingers along his scruff and breathlessly ask, "Maybe you should come inside?"

Seventeen

WOLFIE

As we stumble over the threshold of Penelope's apartment, every nerve ending in my brain is firing with the same persistent message . . .

Let the fuck go.

Let go of the past, of the anxiety, of all the bullshit that's been holding me back from the gorgeous woman in front of me.

I've spelled it all out for her, showing her where I grew up, admitting what happened to me there. And despite it all, she's still here, clutching my shoulders and kissing me with a sense of urgency, like she can't get close enough, like she wants to take on all my pain and help me heal.

It does things to me—warm, soft, sweet things—to know that this gorgeous, perfect girl actually wants *me*.

The door has hardly closed behind us before my fingers are weaving into her soft blond hair, pulling her back into the intoxicating kiss we started in my car. She tastes like honey and early winter air, so sweet and biting all at once.

I've never felt this close to anyone in my life, and not just because she's pressed against my chest, our tongues rolling together in a gentle, rhythmic dance that has every square inch of my body on high alert. No, it's because this beautiful, confident woman knows *me*, all of me, even the ugly parts, and it feels like the first step in letting go of everything.

When we part, I'm breathless and aroused, but I know I need to slow things down, to see where Penelope's head is at. The last thing in the world I want to do right now is rush through this. That's what the old me would have done. The new me I'm still figuring out, but I know he'd want to take his time with this beautiful girl.

She's still touching my cheek, running her palm over the stubble on my jaw. "Hi," she says, smiling.

"Hey," I say with a shaky laugh. "Thanks for inviting me in, for sticking with me tonight."

She nods at my attempt at gratitude. But that's what I feel—grateful. At least for now, it seems that Penelope wants to be the one to help me dig out from under my past.

"Would you like a drink or something? Bottled water? Wine?"

"I'll take a water. Thanks."

I take a seat on the sofa while Penelope retrieves the water from the fridge. Once she hands me the bottle, she settles in next to me.

I have no idea where we go from here, and as crazy as it sounds, I'm terrified of fucking this up. I uncap the water and chug a large swallow, biding my time.

She moves closer and takes the water from my hands, setting it on the coffee table in front of us. I gaze into her wide blue eyes, imagining for just a minute what it would be like to push all my walls down and just be with her.

Penelope trails her fingers through my hair, and my eyes sink closed. "Is this okay?" she murmurs, her voice soft.

"Very," I say with a husky rasp.

When I open my eyes again, she's biting her bottom lip, looking at me like I'm a puzzle she's desperate to solve.

It does things to me. This kind, sweet woman being here with me, willing to try this after what I've just told her. She's so soft and tender . . . *so perfect.*

Her hands trail down my neck, and then she begins rubbing my shoulders. It feels nice.

Don't, Wolfie. I try to remind myself that this is just physical, but I fail miserably. I can tell already that this wouldn't be just sex. I'm already all up in my feels, and we've barely begun.

As I move closer to her on the couch, she tilts her head, lifting her chin so her mouth is only inches from mine. It's the most natural thing in the world to lean in and steal a sweet kiss.

With a soft sound, she leans in, pressing her full mouth to mine.

"Missed you," she murmurs, threading her fingers into the hair at the back of my neck again, using the leverage to pull me in closer and deepen our kiss.

Her words have an immediate effect on my body. When I put my hands on her waist, she crawls into my lap, pressing her warm center into my cock, which strains against my jeans.

Don't think.

And I don't.

I let Penelope grind in my lap, and I kiss her until she's writhing against my erection, making tiny, need-filled sounds.

Fuck. I need to take a breath.

When I gather my senses and suggest, "Let's go to your bedroom," she meets my eyes with a hazy expression and nods.

We make it as far as the hallway before our kiss grows into something more. While I find my grip on her plush ass, she lets one curious hand venture down the front of my jeans, brushing lightly against my zipper.

The déjà vu from earlier this week is very real, and just like before, a twinge of anxiety kicks in my chest. But this time, I have the wherewithal to tell it to shut the fuck up. Nothing is keeping me from this girl tonight. Especially not myself.

"Is this okay?" Penelope murmurs, caressing my length through the denim as she presses a kiss into my neck.

"Fuck yeah" seems like a bit of a jarring response, so instead, I put my answer in the form of an action, rocking my hips into her so she can feel just how hard I am for her. She gasps, then meets my pressure with her own, her hand working me over in firm strokes through my jeans.

Soon my anxiety is miles in the rearview, with nothing but pure, wild want in its place. I want her. All of her. And by the way she's gripping me like I'm a first-place trophy, I'd say she wants the same.

"Bedroom?" I murmur against her lips.

Penelope pulls back, a look somewhere between confusion and lust dancing through her pretty blue eyes. Realizing that we never quite made it yet, she laces her fingers with mine and guides me the last few paces down the hall to her bedroom.

It's just as eclectic as the rest of her apartment. Big framed abstract art prints. A coral quilt draped over the end of her bed, which she pulls me eagerly onto. Our mouths join again, our tongues moving together in easy strokes.

Whatever was broken inside me, she's mending it with every kiss, every soft brush of her fingers along my jaw. But the longer we kiss, the more my erection strains against my jeans, so hard it's bordering on the edge of painful. I need more.

I tug at her sweater, barely choking out my demand. "Take this off for me?"

Penelope arches one eyebrow ever so slightly as she catches her breath. "You sure? You can stop me at any point if you're uncomfortable."

I nod, fully knowing I won't be taking her up on that offer, then peel out of my long-sleeved shirt to show her I'm not fucking around.

I don't want anything between us. No secrets, no dark pasts, and certainly no clothes.

She ditches her soft gray sweater, and I'm pleased as fuck at what's underneath. No bra. Just her perfect, perky tits, her pretty pink nipples that are begging for my mouth.

We come together again, her soft hands clinging to my shoulder as I weigh her tits in my palms. When I drag my thumbs along her nipples, they stiffen into two perfect pink buds, just as responsive as she was the first night we were together.

It's an honor to touch her like this again, and I won't take a single second of it for granted. I'm going to commit every inch of her to memory. I'm going to dream about her in detail for weeks.

"Fuck, these are perfect," I murmur, leaning down to give one budded nipple a gentle lick, and she responds with a gasp.

Fuck, that's sexy.

My chest tightens at the sound, so I capture the other nipple between my lips, hoping for a similar reaction. What I get is even better—my name, low and breathy, tumbling off her pouty lips.

Fuck, if this woman hadn't already knocked all my walls down, they'd sure as hell be crumbling for her now.

"Touch me," Penelope pleads on a whisper, draping one hand over mine and guiding it to the space between her legs. "Please."

Oh, baby. You don't have to ask me twice.

I ease her onto her back and work my way down her rib cage, planting hungry kisses against her sweet skin. She tastes floral, and if I could, I'd freeze time and live here in this moment. But I can't stop time. I can only keep going forward, traveling lower and lower to the spot I want to kiss the most.

When my lips brush against the skin just above the button of her jeans, she shudders beneath me, her hips bucking up, desperate to close the space between us.

God, I want to devour her.

I tug her zipper down and work her jeans off, tossing them to the floor. My body floods with heat when I lay eyes on what's waiting for me beneath.

"You're so sexy," I murmur, brushing the pads of my fingers along the black lace between her thighs, watching her wiggle against my touch.

"Yeah?" She teases, lifting her hips off the bed to help me out.

I love how bold Penelope is, love how she's not afraid to go for what she wants, even if, inexplicably, what she wants is me.

I give the waistband a tug and ditch the damp, lacy fabric at the foot of the bed, then part her with a gentle touch of my thumb. She twitches as I press a finger into her, then contracts when I add a second. She's so wet, so ready for me.

"So good, Wolfie," she says, panting.

But she's the one who's good. Great. Perfect. More than I could ever deserve. I still can't believe she's giving herself to me like this.

I keep two fingers lodged deep and lean forward, my tongue lapping against her in slow, deliberate stokes. She tastes as good as she looks. When my lips seal around her most sensitive spot, she clutches the sheets with her fingers, and before long she's unraveling, quivering and gasping as I suck and kiss and nibble.

"F-fuck, Wolfie," she stutters, breathless.

"You taste so good," I murmur, thrumming my fingers deeper. "Come for me, sweetheart."

"Yes," she chokes out. "Yes."

And then I feel Penelope come apart, her body jolting as she tightens around my fingers.

It's hot as hell, and my cock jerks inside my boxers. I've never wanted anything more than to feel her body contracting and yielding around mine.

As she comes down from her high, I reemerge, admiring her blazing blue eyes as she swipes one sweaty strand of blond hair from her forehead. Her lips part as if to say something else, but after a prolonged silence, all she can get out is a little whimper of pleasure. It's so fucking cute, how lost for words she is. It makes me want to get her off again. Which I intend to.

I join her on the bed, my head sinking into the pillow next to her as I trace delicate patterns on her cheekbone with the tips of my fingers.

I feel breathless, and my balls ache. I've never been this eager to get naked with a woman before, but with Penelope, I am.

I'm still wearing my jeans, but she's rid me of my shirt, and she can't seem to stop rubbing her hands up and down my chest and abs, stopping just before my waistband. I'm not ashamed to say that I'm loving her hands all over me, no matter where they are. It feels really fucking good, and even though I want more, I'm happy to enjoy this moment and go with the flow.

It's a new feeling for me.

Then she reaches between us and unbuttons my jeans, and my heart rate triples.

"Can I touch you?" she asks.

"Yeah," I manage to say, my voice tight.

I kiss her throat as her hands work inside my boxer briefs. I can't stop kissing her, wanting her so badly, I can hardly think straight.

This moment feels so much bigger than it should, like it means something, but I can't help myself. It does. It means the world to me. And if I'm only going to spend tonight pretending this beautiful girl is mine, then I'm going to make the most of it.

She stills unexpectedly. "Wait."

Her expression is slightly worried, and I have no idea what could suddenly have her on edge.

"Should I get a condom?" She bites her bottom lip, looking unsure. "I don't want to assume, but I

. . ."

"I want to be inside you," I say darkly. It's an offer and an admission, the only thing I've been able to think about since I parked my car outside her apartment.

With a small smile, she helps me out of my jeans, my already stiff cock springing free into her palm. She strokes me slowly, all the way down and then back up as a hot breath shudders in my chest. Then Penelope leans to her bedside table and I hear the crinkle of foil. I take the condom and cover myself, and then she's straddling me, teasing the sensitive head by nudging it against her heat. I choke out another gasp.

Before she can continue her maddening cock tease, I roll us over, caging her in with my body so that she's underneath me.

When I push my hips forward, my length slides against her hot flesh, and we let out a simultaneous groan. I rock forward, my cock sliding along her center, drawing lazy circles against her swollen clit.

"Wolfie."

Penelope gasps, her eyes widening as her hands clamber to find their grip on my shoulders. But before she can get another word out, I tilt my hips, sinking into the tightest, most perfect heat I've ever felt.

With our eyes locked, our lips just a breath apart, I give her another inch, then another, testing her limits. Her eyes widen, her grip tightening on my back.

"So deep," she whispers, and I groan in agreement.

She's so small, I'm worried I may break her if I give her all of me. But not a moment later, she's proving me wrong, tugging my shoulders against her until I'm buried within her. I groan, kissing the hollow part of her neck where her collarbone meets her shoulder.

"Fuck, sweetheart. That okay?"

Her eyes open and meet mine, hooded and filled with pleasure. "It's perfect. You feel amazing."

"So do you," I say, my voice tight and raspy.

Pleasure rips through me, racing down my spine. I'm drunk off her. Every sensation is new and different, but is also comforting and familiar in a way I've never experienced before.

I know tonight is different. Penelope is different. I don't have to feel shame and guilt and flee five minutes after I've come.

We work our way into a slow, steady rhythm. I don't want to rush through this. It's a big moment, one I've been waiting a long time for. Maybe my entire life.

We move together, my hips grinding against hers with every thrust, the melody of her moans punctuated with little needy noises. I capture them in my lips, kissing her again and again as my pulse riots.

Fuck, I'm close.

"Wolfie," she says on a low moan, her muscles tensing around me.

She's close too. I can feel it.

Penelope's body is humming beneath mine, every inch of her pulsing with the most irresistible heat. It's perfect, but it's nothing compared to the look on her face. Her full, pouty lips part as she drags in uneven breaths, her eyes half-lidded and filled with lust.

"Wolfie, please, I—"

When I bring one hand between us and touch her clit, whatever she was going to say is replaced with a quick, desperate gasp, accompanied by the feeling of her tightening around me.

Fuck, I'm gonna explode right with her.

With one final moan, Penelope digs her finger-nails into my back, hanging on for dear life as I pump into her, unloading in hot, fast spurts just as she comes undone.

We fall back together in a breathless heap on her bed.

Eighteen

PENELOPE

"Happy birthday, dear Connor. Happy birthday to youuu!"

The flickering firelight of twenty-nine candles dances across my brother's cheeks as our very off-key singing echoes through his kitchen, then fades into a wild round of applause.

"Make a wish, old man!" Hayes shouts, lifting his beer before tipping back whatever's left in the bottle. "You're not getting any younger!"

"But I'm getting hungrier," Caleb shouts. "And I'm gonna eat that cake with my bare hands if you don't hurry up, swear to God!"

Laughter ripples through the group, coming from everyone but the birthday boy himself, who is busy staring into the flames.

"Hold on," he grumbles, furrowing his brow in concentration. "I'm trying to think of a good one."

A jam-packed kitchen and a chocolate cake isn't at all what we had planned for Connor's birthday celebration. Just like every year, we'd planned his annual "Connor Crawl" through a strip of River North bars, complete with T-shirts and a hashtag for posting all our drunken pictures the next morning. If there's one thing my brother loves, it's his birthday, so we always pull out all the stops.

But this morning, we all woke up to a group text from him requesting a quiet night in instead. Despite my suspicions that my wild-child brother had been possessed by a demon, I threw out my Saturday morning plans in favor of baking him his favorite chocolate cake with bright blue frosting, and we all made good on his request.

Well, except for the *quiet* part. The guys seem to be having a hard time getting that suggestion through their heads.

"Tick tock," Hayes teases, letting out a laugh. "Any day now, Father Time."

Connor glances up with a weak smile that doesn't quite reach his eyes.

With each passing second that he stares blankly into the flames, my stomach ties itself into a tighter and tighter knot. I knew something was up when he called off the bar crawl, but my bets were on a slight hangover or a gnarly pimple holding him back.

But from the second I walked through the door tonight, I knew something major was off. All night, Connor has seemed a thousand miles away, even when he's standing right beside me. Like now, his easygoing smile is nowhere to be found, and he's studying those burning candles on the cake like they hold all the answers.

After thirty incredibly awkward seconds of Connor staring down his candles, I reach over and pinch his forearm under the table. "Uh, Connor? Before the wax melts onto the frosting?"

"Oh, uh, yeah. Sorry." He sucks in a big, dramatic breath and proceeds to huff out all twenty-nine candles at once. It would be impressive if it didn't feel oddly reminiscent of a sigh of defeat.

What's going on with him? He's acting like the human equivalent of a glob of melted candle wax in a big bite of birthday cake. Not that anyone other than me seems to be acknowledging that.

"Attaboy, Connor." Caleb claps him on the back with one hand, fanning away the smoke with the other. "Twenty-nine years young and he's still got it."

"Only one more till the dirty thirty," Scarlett says gleefully from beside me. "Someone get this man a walker!"

Connor shakes his head, huffing a strand of his dark blond hair from his forehead. "If you keep giving me shit, I'm not sharing my cake with you," he mutters. "C'mon, let's cut into this thing."

Wolfie flips on the lights and appears with a stack of paper plates and forks, shouldering his way to a spot at the table to help serve up my masterpiece.

Not to toot my own horn, but I managed to pull off a seriously gorgeous cake in Connor's favorite colors with only a few hours' notice. With thick blue piping around the edges and HAPPY BIRTHDAY CONNOR written in a kind of messy script, I might actually fool someone into thinking I bought this at a bakery. Maybe if this promotion doesn't pan out at work, I should pivot to a career as a pastry chef.

"This looks amazing, Penelope," Wolfie murmurs as he slices a knife through the thick layer of frosting, revealing the rich chocolate cake inside. "Almost too pretty to eat."

A chill rolls through me at his word choice. He

sure didn't say that between my thighs last night.

No. Bad Penelope. No sexy thoughts about your brother's roommate at his freaking birthday party. No matter how incredible he was last night.

Wolfie plates an extra-thick slice, then holds it out to me. I happily accept it, enjoying the prickle of electricity dancing along my fingertips when they brush against his. Likely a side effect of the fact that less than twenty-four hours ago, this man had me gripping my bedsheets for dear life.

Admittedly, I'd drag him down the hall and give his bedsheets the same treatment if not for the fact that we'd have quite the audience out here to hear it all. An audience that includes, of course, my brother. Who is still oblivious to the fact that Wolfie and I are anything but friends.

"You're really gonna give the first piece to my sister on *my* birthday?"

Speak of the birthday boy and he shall appear.

Connor tugs my plate out of my hands, giving Wolfie and me some serious side-eye before disappearing into the living room.

Suddenly, I'm struck with a very real, very nerve-racking thought.

Maybe it's not the age thing that's bothering

Connor tonight. What if the reason he's acting weird is because he knows about Wolfie and me? Just the idea sends panic sweeping through me, leaving all my nerve endings raw.

It would certainly explain him canceling the bar crawl, that's for sure, but he probably would have kicked Wolfie's ass halfway to the suburbs by now if he knew the truth about us.

I swallow my panic long enough to help Wolfie serve up and distribute the rest of the cake. Once everyone has a plate in hand, the group spreads out throughout the apartment, breaking off into a handful of separate conversations, any one of which I could easily join. But there's only one person I should be talking to right now.

My brother.

As I head for the living room, Wolfie follows close behind me, and I turn on my heel, gently pressing my palm against his chest for a moment. Not long enough for anyone to notice, I hope.

"Stay here," I whisper. "I need to talk to Connor alone."

Wolfie dips his chin in a firm nod, his gray eyes filled with sweet understanding. "I get it. Good luck."

"Thanks," I squeak back. "I might need it."

In the living room, I find Connor hunched over on the worn leather couch, pushing a glob of frosting around his plate, which is resting in his lap.

"Is buttercream more of a twenty-eight-year-old thing?" I tease.

He snorts, not even glancing up at me. "Nah. Just no appetite, I guess."

Now that's a red flag if I've ever seen one. The man who stole my slice of birthday cake isn't even eating it? He may as well be spelling out SOS in the frosting. But if I'm going to get him to talk, I need to get him totally alone first.

Operation Evacuate Birthday Boy from his Own Party is a go.

I clear my throat, vying for his attention, and set the bait. "So, can I give you your present now?"

As I hoped, it sparks Connor's curiosity. He looks up from his cake, his gaze narrow and probing. "What are you talking about? We stopped giving each other presents back in middle school."

I open my mouth to protest, then pause, smacking my forehead with the heel of my hand. "Shoot, I just remembered I left it in the car. Can you come get it with me?"

Connor frowns, lifting one suspicious eyebrow.

Jeez. Would it kill him to play along for once?

I plant my hands on my waist, popping one hip to the side. "Fine. You can stay here. But if something happens to your little sister on the streets of Chicago at night, just know it's your fault."

As predicted, that's enough to get him up from the couch. Moments later, we're slipping on our coats and heading for the door.

"We'll be back in just a second!" I promise over my shoulder on our way out. And, *God*, do I hope I'm right.

The cold November air hits almost as hard as the irony of the moment—stepping out onto the busy streets of the city just to get a bit of privacy. Chatty, unfamiliar faces wander up and down the block, probably heading toward the same bars we were planning to go to tonight.

But Connor doesn't even notice them. He just squints up and down the street, cringing against the wind. "Where's your car?"

"Nowhere." I push my shoulders back, feeling more than a little proud of myself. "I took the el. I just wanted to get you out here away from everyone else for a moment."

His eyebrows lift as I plant one hand on my hip.

"Now, want to tell me what's going on with you?"

He whips his head toward me, his lips pulled into a tight frown that matches the disapproval in his eyes. "So you dragged me out into the cold, and there's not even a present?"

I resist the urge to roll my eyes. Of course that's what he's hung up on.

"Sorry. That was kinda cruel. But I spent two hours making you a homemade cake today. And now my present is my love and concern. Seriously, Connor." I sigh, mirroring his crossed arms. "You've been acting weird all night. What's going on?"

He lets out a long, slow sigh.

My heart stills as I watch him decide whether to respond. I've never been so afraid to hear the answer to a question. But if he knows about Wolfie and me, I should be the one to take the heat. I'm the reason any of this happened, after all.

Connor pushes out a slow, shaky exhale, his shoulders dropping as he scrubs one hand through his messy blond hair. "It's . . . it's Beth."

A cocktail of relief and pure confusion shoots

through my veins. So it's not me. It's . . . a girl?

"Who's Beth?"

"Exactly. I hardly know her. We met last May at a bar in River North. You might remember her. Brown hair, kind of short."

I chomp down on my lower lip, holding back a laugh. "You're describing literally every girl you've ever hit on."

Connor huffs, shoving his hands so far into his pockets, you'd think he was trying to break through and touch the concrete. "Whatever. The point is, she's pregnant. Six months pregnant."

Oh. Whoa.

My heart outruns my breath, leaving me dizzy and unbalanced. "Is it . . ."

He nods somberly. "The paternity test came back yesterday morning. I'm the dad."

Those last three words lodge in my chest like a pill I can't quite gulp down. *My brother, a father?* My brain won't even fully register the thought.

"What are you going to do?"

"The right thing," he says firmly, his tortured expression fading to give way to a more serious one. "Whatever Beth wants me to do. I want to be involved as much as she'll let me. I mean, Jesus, this is my daughter we're talking about."

A lump of emotion forms in my throat, and I can barely squeak out my reply. "Daughter?"

The smallest smile pulls at his lips. It's the most joy I've seen from him all night, and something inside my chest squeezes.

"Yeah," he whispers. "It's a girl."

Something about knowing the gender makes the whole thing seem much more real. I try to imagine Connor picking out little pink onesies, learning how to master the art of hair bows and playing pretend with Barbie dolls.

It warms my heart, to be honest. He's been such a good big brother to me. I can only imagine that will transfer well to being some lucky little girl's dad. Maybe the circumstances aren't ideal, but a baby is a blessing, no matter what. Plus, I know I could throw a mean baby shower.

Which brings me to my next question. "Do your friends know?"

Connor laughs. "Hell no. But they're sure as hell going to find out when I start shopping for a car seat."

I barely suppress a smirk. "You know you can't

put a car seat on a motorcycle, right?"

He nods. "That's why I sold the bike."

My jaw nearly hits the concrete. The only thing less believable than my brother getting some girl pregnant is him selling his precious motorcycle.

"No way," I whisper, shaking my head.

"Yes, way," he says. "Wolfie's helping me pick out a car. I guess it's time to finally grow up."

Pride swells in my chest, mixing with the rest of the emotions fighting for my attention. Surprise. Confusion. And love. I love my brother. And I'm proud of him. I never envisioned him becoming a single father, but I know that anything he puts his heart into, he'll be great at.

"How are you feeling . . . about everything?"

Connor shrugs and runs one hand over the stubble on his jaw. "Honestly? I don't even know. It's a lot to process."

I nod. "I get that. And you and Beth? Are you . . ."

He shakes his head. "No. She's actually dating someone else. Says she's really happy."

"That's good, I guess."

I can't even begin to imagine the complexity of having a baby with someone, let alone someone who's now dating someone else. What if Connor doesn't like the new guy who's going to theoretically be spending a lot of time around his daughter?

But before I can contemplate it further, he interrupts my train of thought.

"They're both med school students. Beth's going to be a pediatrician. I remember being impressed that she was in med school. We talked about it that night."

I shift my weight. "Was it only a one-time thing between you two?"

He shakes his head. "No. We saw each other for a few weeks. It was casual, kind of a friends-with-benefits thing. She was too busy for anything else, but I was fine with that."

I smirk. Of course he was. My brother the playboy, ladies and gentlemen.

But now it seems he's found out the hard way about where babies come from. I've never dwelled on it, but yes, my brother has had a lot of casual sex. Although I can't help but wonder if maybe those days are behind him.

Nodding gently, I touch Connor's arm. "I know

that no matter what happens, you're going to be an amazing dad."

He swallows hard. "Thanks, Pen."

Before things start getting too mushy between us, I motion back toward his apartment. "All right, let's go enjoy what's left of this party. Gotta live it up for the next three months before your Saturday nights start to look a whole lot different."

He winces. "Do you have to rub salt in the wound?"

"I'm your sister." I shrug. "Isn't that my job?"

Upstairs, the party is still buzzing along like it was when we left it—music playing, friends laughing too loud. But now, with a heavy weight off his chest, Connor is actually able to enjoy his evening. He finally digs into his cake, even going for a second slice, and sips on one of his favorite craft beers while singing along to some old nineties hip-hop song Wolfie included on tonight's playlist.

I can't help my gaze from straying over to Wolfie every so often. He looks like all kinds of naughty fun with his serious expression, dark eyes, and the way his long-sleeved T-shirt hugs his muscular arms and stretches across his chest—a chest that I love burrowing into.

Wait, is *burrowing* the right word?

I don't know, but I do know I love the feel of being in his arms. It's safe and comfortable. A few times during the evening I feel his eyes on me too, and it sends a little thrill zipping through me to think about our secret tryst that no one knows about but us.

There are so many things to like about Wolfie. I like the way he looks at me. The way he listens when I talk, with utter and complete interest in what I have to say. I like that he wanted to take things slow between us rather than rush into bed like a lot of guys would have at my offer. He's thoughtful in everything he does, even if that *thing* is hooking up.

Being with Wolfie, overcoming the obstacles holding him back, watching him open up to me . . . it makes me feel all warm and flushed inside. I know this was only supposed to be about sex, about scratching an itch, but it's not anymore. I'm not sure when things changed, but it's obvious they have.

I might have told him that I didn't have time for a relationship, that I only wanted to exchange an orgasm or two with someone other than my vibrator, but it's already become so much more. And I have no idea what to do with that information.

Does Wolfie want more too? Is he even capable of that right now? And what will we do if and when Connor finds out? Will it ruin everything?

When the rest of the group filters into the living room to encourage this impromptu karaoke, Wolfie grabs my hand, pulling me into the kitchen for our first moments away from prying eyes all evening.

"Is everything okay with Connor?" Wolfie asks, brushing my hair behind my ear and sending a trail of goose bumps racing down my neck.

"It's . . . complicated," I say, lacing my fingers tight into his and pulling him closer. "But it has nothing to do with what's happening between you and me."

"So he doesn't know?" Wolfie lifts one dark brow. "About us?"

I shake my head, trying to ignore how much I love the sound of him referring to us as . . . *us*. "Doesn't seem like it. He's got bigger things on his mind."

More like smaller things. Tiny little third-trimester things. But it's not my secret to share. And to think I was worried my brother's sour mood was about me and Wolfie. We're the least of his worries.

But we'd still be a worry, if he knew.

Wolfie grips my hand a little tighter, letting the other float to the nape of my neck, guiding my mouth to his in a quick, sweet kiss that makes my toes curl in my wool socks.

"Good," he murmurs, his lips buzzing against mine. "That means we can have a repeat of last night sometime soon."

My skin heats beneath his touch at just the mention of last night. I want a repeat. I need a repeat. If last night were a song, I'd let it play and play until I'd memorized every note.

"Soon," I say, touching his scruffy jaw with my palm. "Please."

"Wolfie, get in here!" Connor's sharp voice cuts through the air, and we stumble back from each other in a panic. "Come do a duet with me!"

Our wide, startled eyes meet for a moment before we break into full-on laughter.

"Can't say no to the birthday boy," I remind Wolfie with a waggle of my finger.

He shrugs, a coy smile pulling at the corner of his mouth as he rakes his fingers through his dark hair. "Seems like I also can't say no to his sister."

Nineteen

WOLFIE

"We need to talk."

Never in my life did I think those words would be directed at me from another man. But when I emerge from my bedroom early Sunday morning, that's the first thing out of Connor's mouth. He's leaning against the kitchen counter with a stern frown on his face, already dressed for the day, despite the hour.

I reach inside my athletic shorts to scratch my balls and make my way toward him. I'd say the early-bird routine is out of character for him, but lately, acting strange seems to be my roommate's new normal.

"Are we breaking up?" I smirk at my own joke, stalking past him to flip on the coffee maker.

But Connor doesn't so much as crack a smile. "Knock it off, dude. I'm serious."

Damn. Normally he's the funny guy, not me. Whatever this role-reversal shit is, I don't like it.

I rub the sleep from my eyes with the back of my hand, assessing the kitchen for last night's damage. A few empty cans here, a couple paper plates crusted with cake there. We've done worse. Definitely not the kind of mess that warrants an argument this early in the morning.

"If it's about the kitchen, I'm planning to clean up." I grab a can off the counter, give it a quick shake to verify that it's empty, then lob it into the recycling bin with a crash. "Sorry. Was too tired last night."

"It's not about the kitchen," he grumbles through clenched teeth. "It's about the whole apartment."

I scoff. "You're as capable of cleaning as I am, birthday boy."

The coffee maker beeps like a ref calling a penalty on this petty argument, and I grab each of us a mug from the cabinet. This motherfucker must need caffeine in a bad way. But an IV drip of espresso injected straight into my veins wouldn't wake me up nearly as fast as the next words out of

Connor's mouth.

"I'm moving out, Wolfie. I'm having a kid."

The next few seconds are sort of a blur. Both mugs slip from my hands, and I watch them fall to the floor in what feels like slow motion, shattering on the tile and sending jagged shards and hot coffee bleeding across the floor. "Fucking shit."

I grab a fistful of dish rags and throw them on the mess., but they're nothing more than a temporary bandage to slap on the situation. There's a bigger crisis that needs my attention right now—the shitstorm my best friend just rained down on me in two fucking sentences.

"What the hell are you talking about, Connor?"

He sighs, one hand steadily working a knot out of the back of his neck. "Do you remember Beth?"

Who? A quick flip through my mental Rolodex of girls he's brought home yields zero results.

"Sorry." I shake my head. "Doesn't ring a bell."

"Shit. No one seems to remember her," he says, using the side of his shoe to kick a piece of broken coffee mug toward the epicenter of the mess. "Hell, I might've forgotten about her myself. You know, if not for a little thing called a pregnancy test. She's six months along. It's a girl."

Slowly, the pieces start to fall into place. Selling his motorcycle, and the fact that he's been acting like the walking dead for the last few days. The dude has practically handed me a bouquet of red flags. Still, I couldn't have guessed that *this* is what's had him so off-kilter.

"So you're gonna be involved then?" I pause, then tack on, "As her dad?" I guess I'll need to get used to using that word to describe him. Connor Blake. A dad.

"Yup. We're talking about sharing custody."

The more Connor talks about it, the more his features start to loosen up. I swear I even spot the threat of a smile pulling at his lips. He doesn't seem nearly as bent out of shape about being a dad as he was about keeping this thing a secret.

"You should come scope out this house with me." He digs his phone from his pocket and pulls up a real estate listing, turning his screen toward me. "Three bedrooms. It's out in Oak Park."

I whistle through my teeth, taking in the pale gray brick facade and black shutters. It's like a snapshot out of *Better Homes and Gardens*. "Damn, you come up on thirty years old and suddenly you're moving to the suburbs?"

He rolls his eyes, pocketing his phone before

backhanding my shoulder. I probably deserve that.

"Shut up, dude. It's like thirty minutes away. It's barely out of the city limits."

We spend the next half hour cleaning up the spilled coffee and broken mugs, all the while chatting about Connor's plans for decorating a nursery. I never thought I'd hear my best friend get so stoked about cribs and car seats and all their safety features, but he's clearly been doing his research. By the time we have the kitchen in pre-party condition, he's yammering on like his normal self, the zombie I've been dealing with a distant memory.

"So, yeah, that's the plan," he says, bagging up the last of the party trash. "New place, a baby daughter, the works. Things are changing."

"Sounds like you'll be a damn good dad."

Connor's smile is wide and genuine. "Thanks. I'd like to think so. I mean, hell, I'm a good-as-fuck older brother to Penelope, right? Hopefully there's some carryover."

Just the mention of Penelope makes a knot form in the pit in my stomach.

Fuck. That's right.

In the midst of this little heart-to-heart, I almost forgot who I'm talking to. Connor. Penelope's older brother. And he is a good older brother, like he said. Except that most good older brothers would never let their sisters get mixed up with a guy like me.

And while he's been spilling his guts like I'm his damn therapist, I've been anything but honest with him for weeks. I'm not sure what's worse, a hypocrite or a liar, but I'm pretty damn sure I'm both.

"Speaking of Penelope," Connor says, interrupting my shame spiral. "She's the only other person besides you who knows so far. And Beth, of course, and anyone she's told. But don't go spilling to the guys yet. I'm not ready to hear a whole bunch of opinions on it."

"All good," I say, choking out my response through the guilt rising in my throat. "Take your time."

"Thanks, dude." He smiles, clapping me on the shoulder. "You're the best."

Too bad I feel like the fucking worst.

With the kitchen cleaned up, Connor disappears to his room to hop on a call with his real estate agent, so I head for the shower to try to scrub some of this shame off me. Unfortunately, it's a bit more than skin deep. I keep the faucet turned cold, shuddering against the reality I've created for my-self, the reality I desperately need to escape.

By the time I shut it off and step out, I know what I have to do. There's only one way I'm go-ing to stop my stomach from churning, and it starts with calling Penelope.

"Hey there, hot stuff." Her voice is cheery and sweet on the other end of the line.

Usually, I'd think that *hot stuff* nickname is cute, but right now, it produces instant nausea. *Better cut right to the chase.*

"Can I come over?" I ask gruffly.

"Duh," she says with a laugh. "But only if you bring over my cake stand. I think I left it there last night."

Perfect. A decent excuse to go over there with-out having to lie to my roommate again.

"Sure," I grunt. "Be there in half an hour."

I throw on whatever clean clothes are at the top of my hamper, then grab the cake stand and head for my car. Traffic is light on Lake Shore Drive, which is a once-in-a-blue-moon miracle on a weekend. Nice of the universe to let me have one good thing today.

I'm at Penelope's apartment in record time, and she buzzes me in, greeting me at the door as I come up the stairs. A slouchy gray pajama shirt hangs off her petite frame, covering up most of the tiny sleep shorts she has on underneath them.

God, who gave her the right to look so cute first thing in the morning? Especially right now, of all times.

"Yay, you brought it!" She takes the round dish, then presses up on her tiptoes, leaning in for a kiss, which I barely dodge. It's a shrewd move that instantly makes her pretty blue eyes cloud over with worry. "What's wrong?"

"A lot is wrong," I grumble. "Your brother is gonna be a dad."

Her brows shoot up to her hairline, a hint of a smile ticking at the corner of her mouth. "So he told you? Here, come inside. Let's talk."

She steps back from her door frame, but I keep my feet firmly planted where I stand. I need to keep this short and sweet. Well, as sweet as something so bitter can be.

"Listen, Penelope. We need to talk." I feel like such a jackass parroting Connor's words from this morning, but they're the first that come to mind.

Her reaction isn't as lighthearted as mine was this morning. Her brows furrow into a tight *V*, her lips parting just enough to make me wish I could kiss the confusion right off her face. But I won't. I can't. I came here on a mission, and I'm not going to fail.

"Talk? About what? Please, just come inside," she says, reaching for my hand.

But I pull back, like she'd be hot to touch. And in some ways, she would be. I know how warm and sweet her hand feels in mine. I can't go there right now. Not with her. Not again.

"We have to stop this," I say curtly, dodging her gaze.

"Stop what?"

I gesture to what's left of the space between us. "This. All of this."

Penelope takes a tentative step toward me, chewing nervously on her lower lip. "If you don't want to keep secrets, we could always tell Con—"

I hold up a hand, stopping her where she is. I can't let her get any closer. Not physically, not emotionally, not at all. Her friendship is one thing, but this is headed down a trajectory I can't go down.

"But what about Friday?" she says, frowning.

"When you showed me the neighborhood you grew up in, and we . . . we . . ."

She won't say it, but I don't need her to. I know what happened. We had sex. After I told her I don't sleep with people just for the sake of getting off. I told her that physical shit means more to me. And now I'm going back on my word.

Way to fucking go, Cox.

"Friday was a mistake." The words are directed more at the floor than Penelope. "We can't keep making mistakes on purpose."

When I pull my gaze up to meet hers, I instantly regret it. Her lip is quivering, her eyes barely blinking back the tears.

"I don't understand."

"What's not to get?" I rasp. "I can't fall in love with my best friend's sister."

With that, her tears break through, chasing one another down to her chin. "Y-you were . . . falling in love with me?"

My heart wrenches in my chest. Fuck, Cox. You're just making it harder on the girl. And on yourself.

"It doesn't matter," I lie. "It can't happen."

Penelope doesn't say anything else, but she doesn't have to. The damage is done. I hurt her, just like I always knew I would. I ruin everything I touch, and while I hoped it wouldn't come to this, I can't even say I'm surprised.

My throat feels tight and my heart is pounding unevenly. "I have to go."

Without another word, I turn around and take the stairs two at a time, racing down to the street and back into the cold.

I thought I knew pain, but this is different. Worse. The kind of hurt you can't just bury and leave to rot deep inside you. This is the kind of pain that's going to stare me dead in the eye for weeks, if not months, to come.

I can't help but think that maybe the guilt of lying to Connor wouldn't have been as bad as this, or the misery of admitting the truth to him, even if he pulverized me to a fine dust once he knew.

But hell, I guess I'll never know.

Twenty

PENELOPE

Pardon my French, but this morning fucking sucks.

I didn't even make it to my desk before making a pit stop for an ugly cry in the office bathroom. Shoving open the door, I barely manage to lock myself into the farthest stall before the waterworks start pouring out of me in quick, breathless sobs.

All it took was running into a coworker who asked about my boyfriend to bring on a dozen painful memories of the work retreat, back when treating Wolfie as my boyfriend was nothing more than a game of pretend. Back when all I wanted from him was a purely physical, no-strings-attached, just-for-the-night arrangement. All because I thought it would be fun.

And it was fun, but it was also so much more than that. He let me into his world, and I developed real feelings.

If only I could have stuck to my own boundaries. Maybe I wouldn't be stifling my sobs into toilet paper right now, brokenhearted and cursing whoever thought single-ply tissue was okay. I might as well be blowing my nose with sandpaper.

Happy Monday to me.

God, when was the last time I cried over a man like this? College, maybe? It's certainly been a long time since I've been this emotionally invested in someone. Not that it was ever my intention to get so wrapped up in Wolfie.

To be totally honest, it wasn't even until Friday night that I realized I wanted something serious with him. Something real and lasting. I wanted to be the only one he shared his secrets with, the only girl to cook him pasta and kiss him good night.

And then less than forty-eight hours later, he pulled the rug out from underneath me, and all those dreams came crashing down. Now I feel as broken as I used to think he was, a thought that just makes me cry even harder.

Can you work with me here, tear ducts? I do have a job to get to, you know.

Once I'm all cried out, I spend ten full minutes practicing my fake smile in the mirror and fanning my eyes to try to chase the redness away.

All right. Pep talk time.

If Wolfie could pretend to be my boyfriend for a whole weekend work retreat, I can play the role of *girl who definitely didn't get dumped this weekend* for the next eight hours. I am a strong, independent woman who won't let a boy breaking her heart affect her workday, especially when that promotion could be announced any day now.

I push my shoulders back, release a fluttery breath, and let my fake confidence carry me down the hall and straight into my cubicle.

And then I see it.

Spencer's desk. It's empty.

No freaking way.

I squeeze my eyes shut and open them one at a time, first the left, then the right. Am I imagining things? Or could it really be true? Has my nightmare coworker finally wised up and realized he's garbage at his job and quit on principle? Or maybe David came to his senses and served his nephew his walking papers.

"Hey, Penny, check out the new digs!"

Or maybe pigs started flying and hell froze over.

I swivel around in my pumps, my head snapping in the direction of that terrible, familiar nickname.

There he is. The bane of my professional existence, sitting at a fancy corner desk, a shit-eating grin on his face and a shiny gold nameplate proudly displayed next to his monitor. It reads SPENCER DOUGLASS, SENIOR CONSULTANT.

So, there's that. The corner cubicles are larger and more private, and are only doled out after a promotion.

"Congratulations." I choke out the word, dropping my purse with a thud onto my desk.

Remember my fake smile from before? Yeah, it's long gone now. How am I supposed to even pretend to be happy for him when this is how they decided to drop this bomb on me? No gentle email, no private meeting with David announcing the promotion, nothing?

"Thanks, Penny." Spencer grins and sucks on his teeth in a way that makes me equally angry and nauseated. "Bummer there weren't two open positions. You know, so you could get one too."

I bite hard on my lower lip, nodding as I collapse into my desk chair and boot up my computer, wondering how I can be so hurt and yet so unsurprised. It's not like the Wolfie situation, where he caught me entirely off guard. I should have seen this coming. In fact, I kind of did.

I was ninety-nine percent sure that Spencer would get the promotion, but part of me was still hanging on to that tiny little one percent. The sliver of hope that was certain the company would make the smart choice, not the choice wrapped up in family ties. Still, I knew the odds were high that I'd end up here, stuck as a junior consultant for yet another long, boring year.

I've hardly begun to throw my pity party when I'm interrupted by a presence looming over my cubicle like a bad omen. It's David Douglass, clutching his LIKE A BOSS mug, his mouth pulled into a tight line.

"Good morning, Penelope. I'm sure you've seen Spencer has taken his spot among the senior consultants."

I dip my chin in a quick nod. "Yes, sir. I already congratulated him."

"Sure did!" Spencer pipes up from across the way, holding two thumbs up above his fancy new desk.

God, he's so immature. He may be a senior consultant now, but that's clearly in title only.

Mr. Douglass smiles at his nephew, then turns his gaze back to me. "So we ought to discuss what that means for your career trajectory, Miss Blake."

I shift in my seat, my desk chair creaking beneath me. "Yes, I guess so."

He takes a long sip of coffee, the steam billowing up from the mug. It makes me wonder how he drinks it when it's so hot. Does he burn his tongue and just not care? Or does the man just not have any feelings? Based on the next words out of his mouth, I'd say it's the latter.

"We'd like your desk to be packed up before noon."

"Are you saying . . . I'm fired?" I blink up at him, unable to fully comprehend what's going on.

"We prefer the term *laid off*. *Fired* suggests you did something wrong. The fact of the matter is it's just not profitable for us to keep junior consultants on staff long term." Mr. Douglass's eyes are apologetic, but the words coming out of his mouth are merciless. "Someone from the front desk will escort you out once you're ready."

I nod, choking back the emotion climbing up

my throat. "Sounds good," I lie, and David disappears back into his office.

And just like that, *bada bing, bada boom*. I'm single *and* unemployed.

As I pile my belongings into a big cardboard box, I can't help but wish I could be more like Wolfie. Detached and emotionless. It would make all of this so much easier.

I do a quick lap around the office, saying goodbye to the few friends I have here, then circle back to grab my things. When he sees me packing up, Spencer lifts a hand to me in the most halfhearted wave I've ever witnessed.

"I'll miss ya, Penny."

"It's Penelope," I spit back. There's no point in playing polite anymore now that I'm off the payroll. "And that's funny, because I won't miss you at all."

When I get home, I'm prepared for another full-on sob fest, but to my surprise, the tears never come. Maybe I used them all up this morning. Or maybe any amount of loss I'm feeling over my job is outweighed by the relief I feel knowing that I will never have to interact with Spencer again.

I ditch my business wear for a pair of jeans and

a comfy old sweatshirt, then pull out my phone, scrolling through my contacts. I can't wallow in self-pity all day. I need to get out of the house, talk to someone, do something.

Landing on Connor's contact, I shoot him a text.

What are you up to?

My phone buzzes right away with his reply.

Home inspection at the new place. Can't wait for you to see it.

Can I come check it out?

Aren't you working?

A groan pours out of me. I'm so not ready to have this conversation. He must sense that through some sibling ESP, because before I can respond, my phone buzzes again.

I'll send you the address. See you soon.

Never have I ever pictured my brother living in suburbia.

A penthouse apartment near the lake, maybe. I even could have envisioned him splitting his time between Chicago and a second home on a tropical island, at some point, if Frisky Business hit it really big. But a sensible brick house in Oak Park? I would have lost money on this bet.

As I pull into the driveway, admiring the trim landscaping and tall, shady pine trees lightly dusted with frost, there's no question in my mind as to why he chose this place. With its warm gray-painted brick and sleek black shutters, it looks like a perfect little slice of the American dream. I can just picture Connor pushing a stroller down the hedge-lined walkway, toward a nearby park. It's hard to believe that reality is only three short months away.

"Welcome to the new crib, sis!"

My brother appears in the doorway, beckoning me in with the sort of proud smile only a new homeowner and soon-to-be father could boast.

He has every right to be proud. He's taken a less than-ideal-situation and spun it into gold.

I hurry up the stone walkway and join him inside, slipping out of my shoes and carefully pairing them at the door so as not to track anything onto the pristine hardwood floors.

"This place is gorgeous," I murmur, tipping my head back to admire the vaulted ceilings in the entryway. "Thanks for letting me come see it."

"Thanks for making the drive." He pulls me in for a quick hug, then holds me at arm's length, one brow slightly arched. "Are we going to talk about why you're playing hooky from work?"

"Nope. Don't want to talk about it." I duck out of his grip, shaking my head.

Before Connor can argue, we're interrupted by the sound of a faucet being flipped on and off again and again. I turn toward the kitchen, spotting a small gray-haired man with wire-frame glasses standing over the sink and scribbling onto a clipboard.

"That's the inspector," Connor says. "I basically just have to be here while he does his thing. C'mon, let me give you the grand tour."

Bubbling with new homeowner pride, he leads me down the hall, pointing out the naturally lit dining room, then the cozy den complete with built-in bookshelves and a redbrick fireplace.

Even without furniture, this place feels so homey. I can clearly picture all of us gathering here for a baby shower, spoiling Connor with all the baby gates and board books he never thought he'd need. It's a sweet thought that quickly sours when I remember that Wolfie would be among that group, standing across the room, probably acting like nothing ever happened between us. I shudder, brushing that haunting thought away.

Upstairs, my brother brags about his walk-in closet and the balcony off his bedroom, which overlooks a nearby forest preserve. I nod along with his ramblings, trying not to look distracted. This whole place would make any couple on one of those house-hunting shows drool, but I'm having trouble giving it all the excitement it deserves. My mind is anywhere but here.

"Over here, Penelope!" Connor shouts from the next room over. "This second bedroom is going to be the nursery."

I follow his voice, stepping into a small ballet-slipper-colored bedroom. Connor is standing in the center of it, beaming.

"The previous owners had a baby girl too. How perfect is that? You'll have to help me decorate, but I already have the crib picked out. You won't believe how many mommy blogs I had to scour to find the one with the highest safety reviews."

For the first time all day, I crack a genuine smile. The thought of my big brother being a mommy-blog reader is pure comedic gold. And the more he talks about his new reality, the steadier my grasp on it becomes.

"So, that concludes the tour. What do you think?" He spreads his arms wide, looking like the king of his new suburban castle. "I make moving to the suburbs look pretty damn good, huh?"

"Not good enough for me to join you," I say, planting my hands firmly on my hips. "But you're right. This place is incredible."

Victorious, he pumps his fist in the air, a wicked grin breaking over his face. "Hell yeah. Can you repeat that to Wolfie for me? He gave me so much shit for moving out here."

As if it weren't hard enough to hear Wolfie's name, the thought of talking to him vacuums the air from my lungs.

Now's your chance, Penelope. Time to be honest.

"Speaking of Wolfie." That name is hot on my tongue, warning me not to go any farther. But I'm done keeping secrets. Connor deserves to know. Especially now that it's over and it hardly matters anymore. "Do you remember when you volunteered him to go to that work retreat with me?"

Connor appraises me with a tight frown. "I thought you said you didn't want to talk about work."

"It's not really about work," I say.

"Ohhh-kay then." Both his gaze and his tone are suspicious. "Yeah, I remember. Why?"

I suck in a deep breath, hoping to gather some courage with it. I can't believe I'm really going to do this right now. But then again, I've already suffered two major losses in the last twenty-four hours. What else do I have to lose?

"Well, I, uh . . . I told everyone at work that he was my boyfriend."

Connor snorts, which jolts me. That isn't at all the response I was expecting.

"Nice. I guess that's easier than trying to explain why you're bringing your brother's roommate along."

"Sure, it was easier, at first," I say, chewing my lower lip raw. "And then, well, things started to get blurred between us."

Connor scrunches his brow. "What do you mean . . . blurred?"

Am I really going to have to spell it out for him?

"I started to, you know. Feel things."

For a long, painful moment, the only sound between us is the low hum of the heater and the distant thud of the inspector's footsteps downstairs.

When Connor finally responds, the words come out on a growl. "Do I need to knock that fucker's teeth in?"

"No. Not even close. In fact, I'm the one who initiated things. I didn't think I'd develop real feelings for him, but . . ." My voice drops to a hushed whisper, my gaze dropping to my socks. "But I did."

From the corner of my eye, I watch as Connor's jaw clenches, his pulse thrumming in his neck. "All right. Well. I didn't see that one coming."

"Honestly, neither did I," I say, barely lifting my gaze to his. "But it doesn't matter anymore. We talked about it, and Wolfie's not interested."

My brother bristles, puffing out his chest a little. "Oh, so I *do* have to knock his teeth in."

Despite trying to hold it back, the tiniest laugh slips from my lips. "Please, let the man keep his teeth."

"Fine, fine." He holds out his palms in surrender, the furious look on his face fading into one of curiosity. "So, what happened?"

With one last deep breath, I tell Connor everything—well, almost everything. It's only fair to leave out the not-safe-for-work parts, along with the private details about Wolfie's past. Those aren't mine to share.

My brother nods along, quietly taking in every detail.

Part of me wonders if this was really the right time to tell him. I could have waited until an easier time, like over a few beers or, you know, on my deathbed. But standing in the middle of what will soon be his daughter's room, it's never been clearer. We're adults now. It's time to act like it.

"So, in summary," I say with a sigh, "he's hot and cold. One second he's opening up to me about his past, and the next he's cutting things off between us and saying we can't be together. I can't keep up."

Connor chews the inside of his cheek, staring off into space as he mulls it all over. "You know, that sounds about right for Wolfie," he finally grumbles. "He thinks of himself as the kind of guy you quit on. I don't know all the gory details of his childhood, but from what I understand, his dad never gave a shit, and the few girls he's dated have been the same. It's always been kind of *take it or leave it* with him."

I nod. "That lines up with what he's told me."

"Right. So when people don't give up on him, he does it for them and gives up on himself," Connor says, frowning.

The knowledge of my brother's truth hits me squarely in the chest. "That's so sad. I know he deserves more."

Connor nods. "He's the best guy there is. Too bad he doesn't see himself that way."

"So, what do I do?" I ask on a whisper.

"Simple. Don't give up on him, and don't let him give up on you."

Twenty-One

WOLFIE

It's been almost a full week of living alone in my apartment since Connor moved out, and so far, it's been fucking weird.

Not always weird in a bad way. I'm already seeing the perks of a roommate-free lifestyle.

No one to eat my leftovers or hog all the hot water, for starters. And now that it's Saturday, I do like knowing I won't be shoving my head under a pillow tonight to drown out the suggestive creaking of Connor's bed from the other side of our shared wall.

Jesus, I still can't believe that same man is about to be a father.

But with the rest of the weekend ahead of me and no plans on my radar, part of me wishes

Connor were here to talk me into heading out to the bars, or play me in a few rounds of whatever mindless video game he's hooked on this month. Instead, I'm sinking into my couch with a beer in my hand, saddling up for a quiet night in with me, myself, and I.

A little too quiet, to be honest. The only sound is the low rumbling of the train rolling by every five minutes or so, but you have to strain to hear it.

I considered moving out when Connor did, considered looking for a new place, but there was really no reason to. I can afford the place just fine on my own, and figured I could turn his old bedroom into a guest room, or an office or something.

In a way, it's peaceful being here without Connor. Or it would be, if I didn't hate being able to hear myself think right now. The longer I'm alone, the louder my thoughts get, and they all seem to be saying the same thing.

I miss Penelope. Like, a lot.

As I slouch back into the couch, my mind races through the possibilities of how she's spending her Saturday night. Maybe she's home alone, thinking of me too. More likely, she's out on the town, flirting with some guy who might take her home. The thought makes my stomach churn, but it's how it should be. She deserves someone easygoing and sweet, like her. Someone she doesn't have to keep a secret from her brother.

And that will never, ever be me.

Desperate for a distraction, I reach for the remote to flip on the TV, but come up empty. I don't have a remote anymore because I don't have a TV. That was Connor's, and I've yet to buy a new one to replace it.

I've got to distract myself somehow.

Just then, my phone buzzes with a text. It's from Connor, of all people.

Maybe he's ready to beg me to move back in with him. Or maybe he's selling his TV for a bigger one. A man can dream.

But no, he's just wondering what I'm up to tonight. I guess I'm not the only one still adjusting to living alone.

I tell him I'm free as a bird, and he shoots back a text asking if I want to come try out one of the Oak Park breweries. It's a bit of a drive, but hell, it's not like I have anything else going on tonight, so I tell him to name a place and time and I'll meet him there.

Less than an hour later, I'm pulling into the parking lot of a massive, industrial-looking building.

It looks like a warehouse to me, the sort of place you'd drive right past if you didn't know what you were looking for. But the address matches the one Connor sent me, so I hop out of my car and walk through the tall steel double doors. One step inside, and I'm greeted with the sharp, hoppy smell of craft beer.

Yeah, I've got the right place.

"Over here!" Connor waves me down from a high-top table in the back corner, nudging the beer list my way as I take a seat on the stool across from him. "How's the old place? Miss me yet?"

"You wish," I say with a grunt, hiding any lack of a poker face behind my menu. There's no chance in hell I'd admit to that. "You been here before?"

He shakes his head, scanning the extensive list of options. "The online reviews were good, though, and their IPA won some big craft beer award two years back."

When the waitress comes by, we each order a pint of the award winner.

I slap down my AmEx, insisting I pick up this round. "Least I can do, since you'll be blowing all your money on diapers pretty soon."

He chuckles and shakes his head. "Thanks, man."

While we wait for our drinks, Connor fills me in on some parenting book he's been reading, which as far as I know is the first book he's read since high school English class. Before long, the waitress is back with two frothy pint glasses filled with liquid gold.

Connor lifts his glass. "Cheers."

I gently tap mine against it, careful not to spill before lifting it to my lips. It's damn good. But I've hardly taken two sips before Connor opens his mouth, and suddenly, the taste in mine turns sour.

"So, Penelope told me what went down between the two of you."

My throat tightens around the lump of nerves that's suddenly blocking my airway, like a boa constrictor squeezing the life out of its prey. I can feel all the blood draining from my face as I stare deeply into my pint glass, summoning whatever part of my brain is responsible for reminding me to breathe, to wake the fuck up and do its job.

"How, uh, how much did she tell you?" I barely choke the words out, then suck in a much-needed breath, my lungs stinging as they expand.

Shit. Pull it together, Wolfie.

"Breathe, dude," Connor says.

As if I'm not fucking trying. What do I usually do when I feel like this? Run? Fat chance of that right now. My legs feel like spaghetti noodles.

Spaghetti. Which just makes me think of Penelope and her homemade pasta sauce.

Shit, I've got it bad.

"Wolfie. Look at me. I'm not mad at you."

Per his request, I raise my eyes to meet his, and am surprised to see him smirking around his pint glass as he takes a long, drawn-out sip, then sets his beer down on the wood-topped table with a *thunk*. "I didn't invite you here to rip your balls off, dude. Relax."

I force a laugh, but it comes out just as awkward and shaky as I feel. Not at all convincing. "If you say so. Still, I'm sorry."

"For what?" he asks. "Sorry you got involved with her?"

"No. I'm sorry I wasn't honest with you. And

sorry I hurt her. That wasn't my intention."

"I think people rarely intend to hurt other people. But they still end up hurt, and we still have to be responsible."

I nod solemnly. No one understands hurt better than me.

"She told me how it started—that at that work retreat, she played you off as her boyfriend."

I nod. "That was surprising."

Without my permission, a small chuckle escapes my lips. She was so brazen back then. So sure about what she wanted. To my shock, it was me.

Although, to be fair, maybe I shouldn't have been so surprised. I'd noticed the way Penelope's gaze seemed to be drawn to me whenever we were in the same room, how her eyes would wander to my lips when we spoke. I just kept telling myself I was imagining it, that there was no way a girl like her could be interested in a guy like me.

Connor leans forward. "So, why'd you cut things off?" he asks, one brow arched.

I bite the inside of my cheek until my mouth fills with the taste of blood. I want to lie. Or better yet, I want to get up and get the fuck out of here.

But something has me rooted to this bar stool. For the first time in too damn long, I'm not going to run. I'm going to be honest.

"Listen, you know how I am," I say, focused more on my beer than on Connor. "I'm complicated. She doesn't need that kind of shit in her life."

"You're right," he says bluntly.

Surprised, I recoil. That wasn't the response I was expecting. "I am?"

"Sure." He shrugs, wiping beer foam from the edge of his glass with his thumb. "If you're going to be so hot and cold, back and forth, then that's complicated. She doesn't need that. What she *does* need is someone to be good to her, make her happy. You did that, from the sound of it. But you've got to stop running from her and then crawling back. Stay and commit, or walk away. Those are the only two choices. What's it going to be?"

The question hits me like a sucker punch to the gut. "I can't be with your sister," I grumble. "It's not fair to you."

"No, what's not fair is you giving her mixed signals, and me having to defend the fact that you're a good guy. Which you are, Wolfie. You know that, right?"

My stomach twists. Shit. Do I know that?

I've always thought I was all right, good enough to get by. But good enough for someone like Penelope? Not a chance. But that doesn't seem to be what Connor thinks. Or what Penelope thinks. So, maybe I should stop thinking it too.

Before I can say a word, Connor's eyes narrow as he pushes his beer aside and plants his forearms on the table. "Look. Shoot me straight. Do you care about her?"

"Of course I care about her," I say quickly.

"No, dude. Do you *care* about her? Don't make me get all mushy-gushy about it."

I gulp down air, settling the fear and guilt in the pit of my stomach with every breath. "I was falling for her, Connor."

"Then stop making it more complicated than it needs to be."

I take another long gulp of my beer, eyeing Connor from behind my glass. "Since when are you so wise about this shit?" I don't say the rest of what I'm thinking, which is . . . *Why aren't you mad? Why aren't you threatening to cut my balls off?*

He smiles and lifts a shoulder. "Maybe I'm just

practicing my good, fatherly advice. You're one of the good ones, Wolfie. I trust you with my sister, man. And you deserve to be loved and to be happy."

The words send a twinge to my gut. Maybe if my dad had been the advice-giving type, I would have had an easier go of things. What I wouldn't give to turn back the clock and tell teenage Wolfie the same thing Connor just told me.

But I can't. All I can do is take his advice and run with it.

And I know exactly where I'm running.

Once the tab is squared away, I thank Connor for his words of wisdom, then rush to my car, routing my GPS straight to Penelope's apartment.

It's not until I'm looking for parking outside of Penelope's place that it occurs to me how bold I'm being. Hell, there's a very high likelihood that she's not even home.

The thought of her chatting up some guy at a bar downtown comes to mind, and my heart kicks in protest. All I can do is hope and pray it's just a thought, not a reality.

By some miracle, I nab a spot at the end of her

block, which should be almost impossible at this time of night on a Saturday. I know better than to take it as a good sign, though. I don't believe in signs or luck or any of that bullshit. But I do believe in me and Penelope, so I race down the block, drawing cold air into my lungs as I stop in front of her apartment building and slam my thumb on the buzzer.

"Hello?" Her voice is soft on the other end of the intercom.

Just one word from her and relief pulses through my veins. *Thank fuck she's home.*

"Penelope. It's me. Can I come in?" I ask, but it's quiet for too long.

Fuck. I should have lied and said I was a pizza delivery guy or something. At least that would have gotten my foot in the door.

But then I hear the latch of the door click open and the low hum of the buzzer allowing me in. She'll see me. It's a start.

I take the stairs two at a time up to her apartment, where she's ready to greet me from behind a crack in the door.

"What are you doing here?" she asks, opening it wider.

There's a judgmental edge to her voice, which I can't blame her for. Last time I showed up at her door, the conversation was an ugly one.

She lets out the slightest yawn, covering her mouth with her palm. "It's late."

I glance at my watch, then lift a brow at her. "It's barely ten o'clock."

"Really? Oops." The faintest blush creeps over the apples of her cheeks.

God, she's adorable. All rosy-cheeked and ready for bed. But I can't get distracted by how cute she is. Not when I have much more serious topics in mind.

"Can I come in?"

Her gaze drops to her fuzzy pink slipper socks, then wanders back up to meet mine. "I'm not exactly dressed for company."

"You look perfect."

Hesitant, she chews her bottom lip for a moment, then pulls open the door. "Come on in."

In the kitchen, I take a seat at her table, and she offers me a mug of tea, which I take her up on. I could probably use something stronger. Liquid courage and all that. But maybe it's for the best that I'm completely sober as I say this.

"I saw Connor tonight," I say hesitantly.

She blinks at me in surprise, obviously wondering where this conversation is going. That makes two of us, since I'm honestly not even sure what to say.

"We met for a beer near his new neighborhood."

Penelope nods. "That's nice."

I take a breath and meet her eyes. They're guarded. Unsure. And I hate that I put that look in her eyes. She used to look at me with such hope, such wide-eyed optimism.

"He mentioned something." My chest feels tight, like I can't quite get enough air. I don't know how to say this next part, so the words fall ungracefully from my mouth. "You told your brother about us."

She frowns as she sets my mug in front of me, then settles in with her own. "Is that a problem?"

"It should've been," I say honestly. "When he started talking, I thought he was going to castrate me. Which I probably would've deserved, with what I've put you through."

She barely hides her smirk behind her pink ceramic mug. "I'm not sure I'd go that far."

"I would. I've put you through hell."

"You've been through hell yourself," she says, pausing to sip her chamomile, still watching me over the rim of her mug. "Connor and I talked about that too. It helped a lot."

My eyes widen.

Wait, what? Never did I expect Connor Blake to actually be helpful in my effort to win over his sister, but wilder things have happened, I suppose. Like me falling for her in the first place.

"What did he say about me?" I ask.

"That you're used to people giving up on you. And that I could be the one to break that pattern."

"Damn."

"Is it true?" she asks, her voice small.

"Maybe." I reach across the table, taking her soft hand in mine.

Lucky for me, she doesn't pull away. Instead, she squeezes tight onto my thumb, like she's not going to let go. And I hope she never will.

"Listen, Penelope. I've always seen myself

as so complicated. Too complicated. For you, for anyone. Thought I'd just be better off alone, not imposing my bullshit on anyone."

"You're not too complicated for me, Wolfie," she says earnestly, blinking up at me with her sweet turquoise eyes.

It's almost too much for me. I'm not used to feeling so much, but with her, it's like my heart's wide open and there's no place to hide.

"You're kind and generous," she says, "and despite what you think, you're a good man."

I swallow. "I'm trying to understand that. To learn to accept my past and move forward with my future. And there's no version of that future I can imagine without you."

Her pretty pink lips barely part as she draws in a quick, shaky inhale. "How am I supposed to know you're not just going to run away again?" She ducks her head, staring deeply into her mug, as if the answer were buried in there somewhere.

I don't know how to convince her, to assure her that I'm not going to pack up and leave again. I've done an awfully good job of tarnishing my track record thus far. What can I say? What can I do?

"Move in with me." The words fall from my

lips faster than I can stop them, but once they're out, I realize just how much I mean them.

Penelope, however, is rightfully confused. She recoils, pure shock draining the color from her face. "What? You're insane."

"No, I'm in love with you. And I don't want to live alone when we could be there together. That's how serious I am, Penelope. I want you with me, all the time, twenty-four/seven. Move in with me."

Her features soften, and something beautiful and sweet shimmers in her eyes. "You're . . . you're in love with me?"

I can't help the smile teasing my lips. "Isn't it obvious?"

Sliding her mug aside, she pushes to her feet and leans over her tiny kitchen table, capturing my lips with hers. She tastes even sweeter than I remember. Like flowers and honey. Like my future.

Like home.

"I love you too, Wolfie," she murmurs against my lips, then pulls back, leveling me with a dose of reality. "But can we at least wait until my lease is up before we talk about moving in together, though? Take things one step at a time?"

"Of course." I nod. "Anything you need."

She arches one mischievous brow, her wild eyes flickering. "Anything?"

"Anything." I laugh, pulling her lips back to meet mine. "I'm following your lead."

Twenty-Two

PENELOPE

Tonight, Wolfie Cox is all fire, no ice.

"What changed?" My question is soft, barely above a whisper. I don't want to question Wolfie, but I do want to understand him.

He gives me a soft look. "I realized there were two paths in life."

"Two?"

He nods. "My path or theirs."

"Theirs?"

He jerks his chin toward the windows. "Theirs. The world's."

"I see. And what have you decided?"

He pauses momentarily, eyes still trained on

the windows. My heart rate increases as I wait, wondering what he'll say next, what he's chosen and trying to figure out why it means the world to me. But it does. I want so much for Wolfie to be free from whatever baggage is holding him back from living his life to the fullest.

"I've decided that it's my life, and it's the only one I've got. And that just because some shitty things happened, I won't give up or quit trying. I want to live, I want to be happy. I want to be with you, Penelope, even if I don't deserve you."

"You deserve the whole world, Wolfie. And I'd give it to you if I could. You're an incredible man."

He smiles and takes a step closer. "Will you go down this path with me then? I can't promise it won't get a little bumpy along the way."

I reach for his hand and when our palms touch, I lace my fingers with his. "No matter how bumpy things get, I'm here. We'll ride out any storm together."

"I'd like that very much."

He levels me with a deep gaze that I feel deep inside my soul.

I could feel it from the moment he showed up at my doorstep, his gray eyes blazing with a certainty

I've never seen from him before. And again in my kitchen, when he spoke in a voice so unwavering, I would have thought he'd always been this sure. Of himself, of us, of everything.

He wants me. He loves me.

And now, tumbling through the doorway of my bedroom, his touch is hot on my skin, lighting little fires in my belly with every brush of his lips against mine. And with him, I've never been so eager to step into the flames.

"Fuck, you're stunning," he murmurs, trailing the back of his fingers along my cheek, moving to the base of my low ponytail, which he tugs loose, casting the band aside.

My hair tumbles over my shoulders, tousled and messy, much like everything about me tonight. But Wolfie doesn't seem to mind.

He takes me in with a soft smile, his wide eyes blazing bright in the early winter darkness. "I can't believe you're mine."

Before I can reply, he pulls me against him, his hold so tight that I can feel our heartbeats colliding with each other as our lips meet. Our kiss is slow and soft at first, as though we might break, then quicker and hotter, like wildfire. Unpredictably hot.

With his mouth sealed to mine, he walks me backward until my knees buckle against the bed, my shoulders sinking softly into the duvet. The shock sucks the air from my lungs for a moment, the same length of time it takes for him to peel off his soft cotton shirt and throw it aside.

I press up onto my elbows to watch him with wide, curious eyes, my heart thrumming out a steady, driving rhythm in my chest.

God, he's gorgeous. All soaked in moonlight, like something from a dream.

Wolfie's broad silhouette is backlit by the hallway light, giving him an almost otherworldly glow. I watch with wonder as he climbs over me, slipping deeper into shadow as he draws closer and closer. By the time his lips meet mine again, I can hardly see him in the darkness. But I don't have to. He's right here, within my desperate grip, slowly grinding his hips against mine.

"I want you." His voice is a low growl against my neck that reverberates all the way to my toes.

"I'm yours," I whisper back. My fingernails dig deeper into the muscles of his shoulders, showing him just how much I mean it. I'm his, only his, and I won't let him slip away from me again.

After planting one last maddening, open-mouthed kiss against my neck, he pulls back long enough to shove his jeans off, letting his boxers go with them. He stands there for a moment, all naked and draped in shadow like a stormy-eyed god, and I fist one hand into my sheets, trying desperately to hold time still.

I never want to forget how he looks right now, all his clothes and walls stripped away. This is Wolfie. And he's sharing himself freely with me. It's the only version of him I want from now on.

He helps me out of my clothes with the quick eagerness of a little kid unwrapping a present on Christmas morning, tossing my sweatshirt and pajama pants off to God knows where. That's a problem for later. Right now, it's just him and me. The two of us, a mess of wandering hands and greedy mouths, taking in every bit of each other that we can.

He moves over me again, and I run my palm along his length, feeling him grow against my touch. He sucks in a sharp breath, then releases it on a low, throaty hum. "Fuck. So good."

"Yeah? This is okay?"

He swallows hard and nods. "More than okay, babe." His eyes close, his hips lifting to meet my strokes with slow thrusts until he's fully hard in my fist.

"I want you inside me," I say, my voice low as I grip his base and guide him right to where I need him most. He's barely touched me, but I'm already wet and ready.

He groans, replacing my hand with his and tracing maddening circles around my clit with the tip of his cock. It's enough to drive a girl absolutely wild.

"Please, Wolfie." I gasp, clutching his shoulders with trembling fingers.

He quiets me with a firm kiss as he shifts his weight, bringing one hand to the needy space between my legs. One finger pushes into me, then another, pumping in and out, deeper and deeper each time, commanding every muscle in my body to clamp down on him. When he curls his fingers against my most sensitive spot, a desperate, breathy moan escapes my lips, my body writhing beneath him as I ride out the wave of an orgasm so intense, it leaves me in a heap.

"So perfect," he whispers against my neck, and I can hear the smile in his voice. "Did you think I wasn't going to get you off first?"

He quickly retrieves a condom and sheaths himself, then lifts my leg over his hip, pressing into me only an inch. Just enough to feel me quiver around him. No time for me to catch my breath. He's giving me what I want.

"I love you, Penelope," he whispers, his eyes unwaveringly trained on mine.

"I love you too, Wolfie."

And then he sinks into me, every inch of him, claiming what's his. Tonight, tomorrow, forever.

My breath stills for a moment, then pours out of me in a low moan of pleasure. *Holy shit, he feels incredible.*

My back bows as I chase his thrusts with my own, and he drives deeper and deeper, bringing me more and more bliss. I can feel myself getting close again, inching toward my edge, and by the way his jaw clenches, I know I'm not the only one.

"Gonna come soon," he warns on a low growl.

"Mm-hmm. Me too, baby."

The words have hardly left my lips when the heat takes over, pulsing through me in white-hot waves. I'm still riding my high when I feel him release, giving a few final thrusts into me before collapsing in a heap at my side, our desperate lungs competing to suck the oxygen out of the room.

"Fuck, Penelope." Wolfie pants out the words, pressing the softest, sweetest kiss against my temple. "You're perfect, you know that?"

But I don't respond. I'm too busy curling into him, resting my head on his chest, listening to the whooshing thump of his heartbeat. And soon I'm slipping into an easy, blissful sleep.

In the morning, I squint awake to the sun reflecting off a layer of freshly fallen snow and directly into my eyes.

I pull my covers over my head, temporarily confused as to why this is a problem for the first time ever. The sun never wakes me in the morning. I sleep on the side of the bed farthest from the window for that very reason.

And then it all starts coming back to me.

Why am I on this side of the bed? Because last night, I sacrificed my usual side of the mattress for a man who I'm pretty sure I can now officially refer to as my boyfriend. Waking up with the sun is a very small price to pay for an evening of multiple earth-shattering orgasms and all-night spooning.

Worth it? Duh.

I shake off my sleepy haze with a yawn, silently praying that my bedmate is already awake too. I wouldn't mind a few sleepy kisses that might lead to something more. Sort of a redo of our morning at the lake house, minus the part where my brother barged in.

But then I roll over, and instead of finding a sleepy Wolfie next to me, there's only the rumpled, empty sheets still barely holding his warmth.

My heart squeezes like a stress ball in my chest, a combination of confusion and heartache falling over me like a heavy fog. He left? Even after he promised that he wouldn't run away again?

I groan as I turn onto my stomach, burying my face in my pillow to hide from this horrible reality.

Stupid, Penelope. Did I really think he meant it this time?

Before I can fall too deep into my pity party, a whiff of something bitter hits my nose, even through the buffer of my pillow.

Is that . . . coffee? It can't be.

I perk up a bit, giving the air another sniff.

Yep. That is definitely coffee.

A second later, the crackle of bacon popping in

a pan echoes down the hall. Relief courses through my veins, and I heave out a full-body sigh.

Thank God. Not only is Wolfie still here, but he's put himself to work in the kitchen. I guess miracles do happen sometimes.

Slipping out from beneath the sheets, I find last night's clothes, which we so sloppily discarded on my bedroom floor in the heat of the moment. Both my sweatshirt and my pajama pants have to be flipped right side out again, and after a minute or two of searching beneath the bed, I officially have no clue what happened to my slipper socks. I pull a fresh pair from my dresser, sliding them onto my feet before padding out to the kitchen.

There, I'm greeted by a shirtless Wolfie, his muscular back turned to me as he adjusts the burners on the stove like a well-practiced DJ. Except instead of cooking up club beats, he's making bacon and eggs. Which, in my opinion, is a zillion times better.

"Good morning," I murmur sleepily, wrapping my arms around his trim waist and resting my cheek between his shoulder blades. Even when we're standing up, this man makes the best human pillow ever.

"Mmm, morning, cutie." His back muscles flex

as he slides a perfectly fried egg onto a plate and then turns to give me a hug. "Sorry for raiding your fridge."

"No apologies necessary, as long as you're sharing."

His laugh rumbles through him, low and gritty. I can feel it buzzing against my cheek. "Of course. I'll be done cooking in a minute, if you want to pour yourself some coffee." He tips his head toward the coffeepot, where there are already two mugs waiting for us on the counter.

My heart squeezes again, but this time, it's from pure bliss.

Homemade breakfast, a fresh pot of coffee, and I get to put my feet up? I could definitely get used to this.

I pull my favorite French vanilla creamer from the refrigerator door, then settle in at the table to enjoy the view of this gorgeous man cooking for me.

"Is this all part of your grand plan to get me to move in with you?" I tease.

He glances over his shoulder, one thick brown brow arching in playful curiosity. "Why, is it working?"

I nod, holding up one finger for him to wait as I take my first sip of coffee. "But I meant what I said about finishing up my lease first."

"And I meant what I said about giving you whatever you need."

A coy smile pulls at my lips as I eye the crispy strips of bacon sizzling in the pan. "I think what I need right now is some of that bacon. Like, as soon as possible."

Wolfie laughs, a deep throaty sound that makes me smile. Then he grabs the tongs and piles a hefty stack of bacon onto each plate, along with eggs for each of us.

"A girl who knows what she wants," he says, setting a full plate in front of me. "That's exactly what is going to get you that promotion at work."

With that, my smile disappears, and my appetite goes with it. I guess we're having this conversation now. "Um, actually, I have to tell you something."

He sets down his plate and leans against the counter, giving me his full attention. "Yes?"

"I, uh . . . I got fired, actually," I mutter, my cheeks flushing hot with embarrassment. "Spencer got the promotion—surprise, surprise—and I ended up on the chopping block."

It takes a good long moment and a few cleansing breaths before I have the guts to look up from my plate and gauge Wolfie's reaction. His frown is dark, both sympathy and frustration etched on his handsome face.

With a grunt, he folds his arms over his bare chest and shakes his head. "What a load of bullshit. That dude is a lazy prick."

"Tell me about it." I sigh, reaching for the creamer and adding another generous splash to my coffee. Anything to sweeten the bitterness of the situation.

"Well, you'll find something better," he says, his voice level and certain. "There's got to be a thousand jobs in this city for someone as smart as you."

Wolfie sounds so sure, so convinced about this, for a second I actually believe him. But then I remember the fruitless hours I spent scrolling through job search sites last night before he arrived, and my confidence drains again.

I lift a shoulder, drawing lazy circles in my coffee with my spoon and watching as it turns from light brown to a creamy tan. "I know I'll find something eventually, but right now, I just feel so disposable."

"You're not disposable," he growls. "Not even close. You deserve a job where your talent is recognized. I can take a look at your résumé, if it would help."

"Or you could just find a job for me?" I offer him a weak smile. "Can that be part of the whole *winning me back* thing too?"

Wolfie shakes his head. "No way, babe. You don't need me for that. This is your career. You can do this on your own. And I know you will."

His confidence in me is inspiring.

I sigh, then bite into an extra-crispy piece of bacon to keep myself from arguing about this. I know he's right, even if I don't want him to be.

Just like I can't solve all his problems, he can't solve all of mine. But we can be there for each other. I guess that's the silver lining in all of this. I won't have to go through it alone.

"I just wish for once something in my life could be easy, you know?" I wave the remainder of my piece of bacon through the air, then polish it off in three quick bites.

Wolfie grins as he slides into the seat next to mine, giving my thigh a reassuring squeeze beneath the table. "Take it from someone who has never had it easy. It sucks a lot of the time, but it's worth it to fight for what you want."

"I guess if there's anyone who knows about that, it's you."

He grunts. "That's for fucking sure. Come on. Let's eat before these eggs get cold."

We make quick work of our breakfast, all the while chatting about my career, my lease, all the big, ambiguous things about my future.

After all of the digging around in the past we've done together, it's refreshing to start looking forward. To hear Wolfie talk about his goals for Frisky Business, for himself, for us as a couple . . . it's not just encouraging, it all seems so attainable. When he swears up and down that I'll get a new, better job and we can start saving for a condo somewhere on the north side, it doesn't sound like a fantasy. It sounds like a plan. And I can't wait for that plan to start unfolding.

By the time breakfast is done, the time on the clock on the stove is inching dangerously close to eleven o'clock. As much as I'd like to drag Wolfie back to my bedroom and spend the day laughing and kissing and planning our future together, the calendar on my phone says that's not in the cards.

"I hate to say this, but I'm going to have to kick

you out pretty soon," I say. "I've got plans with Connor."

Wolfie raises his brows at the mention of my brother.

"I promised him I'd swing by his house and help him assemble the crib he just bought. You know how he is . . . Mr. I Don't Need to Look at the Directions."

My bubbly laugh mixes with Wolfie's gritty one, a perfect dissonant harmony.

"I'll let you get to it," he says, pressing up from his seat. "Can I see you soon, though? Tomorrow night?"

"Sounds perfect. Your place?"

Wolfie lifts a brow, a devilish glint dancing in his stormy eyes as he tugs on his coat. "Why? Trying to check out your future apartment?"

I roll my eyes, but the smile tugging at my lips is a dead giveaway. The thought of moving in with him is growing on me a little too quickly. "You're never going to drop that, are you?"

He shakes his head. "Nope. Gonna keep saying it till it's true."

Between you and me, I suspect that won't be

long at all.

Twenty-Three

WOLFIE

"**K**eep going, just a few more blocks this way."

Penelope guides me down the pine-tree-lined streets of Oak Park, directing me from memory toward Connor's house. She's been to his place plenty of times since his move, helping with home decor and crib assembly and everything in between.

But this is only my second time out this way, the first being my trip to that brewery with Connor a few weeks ago. I know about as much about navigating suburbia as I know about landing a plane.

"This one right here. Make a right."

She points me down a side street, and as I turn, I notice her legs bouncing absently beneath the tin-foil-wrapped cake in her lap. It's pretty fucking adorable, although I hope it's from excitement, not nerves.

Penelope has been planning this baby shower all month, stressing over catering details and picking out the perfect decorations. If party planning weren't enough of a stressor, there's also the added layer of knowing that this will be our first time hanging out with our friends since making our relationship official.

It's a big day for a lot of reasons, but surprisingly, I'm feeling pretty at ease about the whole thing. I guess that's just the effect Penelope has on me. Having her by my side makes everything else seem a whole lot less scary.

I slow the car to a crawl, squinting out the window at the house numbers to find the one that matches the invitation. When I spot the gray brick house at the end of the block, though, I don't even have to double-check. That's definitely the same house from the real estate listing Connor showed me. Only now it has a lot more meaning than some picture on a home browsing website. It's Connor's first real home, and I can't wait to help him christen the place.

I pull off to the side of the road, joining the half dozen other cars that are already parked here, most of which I recognize as belonging to our friends. The black sedan with the vanity plates assures me that Hayes is here already, which is good. He and Maren were on decoration duty. Caleb's car is here and Scarlett's is too, her front right tire halfway up onto the curb. She's never been the best driver.

I park behind her, then hurry out of the car to help Penelope with the door. Yes, I'm a gentleman, but mostly, I don't want to risk anything happening to that beautiful cake she made. One wrong step on the ice and *bam*, cake meets snow.

Gingerly, Penelope passes off her handiwork to me, then grabs our presents from the back seat. One for Connor and one for Beth, the mother-to-be. They're getting identical sets of burp cloths today, but there's a top-of-the-line bouncy seat set to be delivered to Connor's house at the end of the week, compliments of Aunt Penelope and Uncle Wolfie.

We head down the street, side by side, and travel up the stone walkway to Connor's front door. He really nabbed a fine piece of real estate here. And the light pink baby shower decorations on the porch give it a little extra dash of curb appeal.

"Don't bother with the doorbell," Penelope tells me, shifting the gift boxes into one hand and reaching for the door with the other. "I've been letting myself in for weeks." Just as her fingers hover above the door knob, she hesitates and turns back to me, her pretty blue eyes brimming with concern. "Wait. Pause. Are you okay?"

Confused, I bristle. "Do I seem like I'm not?"

"I just mean . . . are you nervous? I probably should've asked if being a couple in front of all our friends was okay with you? Not nervous?"

She chews her lower lip, and I wish more than anything that my hands were free to pull this kind, thoughtful woman into my arms and kiss the worry out of her. But I can't, so instead I lean down and press my lips between her furrowed brows.

"I'm not nervous, sweetheart," I assure her. "Not with you by my side."

Her features soften, a warm smile forming on her cherry-red-painted lips. They're so vibrant against the dull gray colors of December. But that's Penelope for you. Bright and wild in an otherwise dull world.

"You're sure you're okay?" she asks again. "You're not just saying that?"

"The only thing I'm nervous about is getting this gorgeous cake you made into the house safe and sound," I say, nodding toward the precious foiled-wrapped cargo in my hands. "Everything else is under control. Come on, babe. Let's do this thing."

Inside, the house is buzzing with chatter, and I follow Penelope down the warmly lit hallway to the living room, where the party is centralized. All the usual suspects are gathered around the do-it-yourself nacho bar, a grand slam of a catering decision on my girlfriend's part, in my opinion.

Hayes and Maren nailed their job as party decorators, placing bouquets of bubble-gum-colored balloons in every corner and hanging silver streamers around the bay windows.

The star of the show, however, has to be the hand-painted sign that Penelope had custom made for the buffet table. It reads NACHO AVERAGE BABY SHOWER, which is both funny and painfully accurate, seeing as Connor, his baby mama, and his baby mama's new boyfriend are all in attendance today. You know, just the classic, all-American family. Although, to be honest, it's kind of awesome at the same time.

"Penelope! Over here!"

Maren waves my girlfriend over to the gift table, leaving me alone with this precious frosted masterpiece. I recruit Caleb to help me shift the tortilla chips and salsa to make room for the cake at the end of the buffet, and I don't even realize I'm holding my breath until after I've peeled back the layer of tin foil.

Whew. Thank God. It looks just as perfect as when we left my apartment. The fuchsia frosting is totally untouched, and the words IT'S A GIRL! didn't get so much as bumped.

"Is this your work?" Caleb asks, gesturing to the cake.

I snort. How kind of him to think I'd be capable of this sort of thing. I'm liable to fuck up making brownies from a box.

"Nah. That's all Penelope. She's some sort of cake-decorating sensei. Just one of her many talents."

I'm glad she's off chatting with the girls and not around to hear me brag about her. She'd probably get bashful about it and roll her eyes at me. But I can't help it. I've yet to find anything this girl isn't good at. Wherever she lands in her next professional role, I know she'll absolutely crush it.

Caleb slips off to the kitchen muttering something about finding a serving knife, and I scan the room for the dad of honor. Instead, I spot an unfamiliar couple tucked back in the corner. The woman has mid-length brown hair, her butter-colored dress stretched tight over a big round baby bump.

I'll bet I can guess who that is.

After taking advantage of the nacho bar, I make my way over to introduce myself. "Nice to meet you. I'm Wolfie. You must be Beth." I extend a hand to her, giving a friendly nod to the tall man beside her.

"How'd you guess?" She smirks, running a hand along the top of her bump. "And this is my boyfriend, Brett. Brett, this is Connor's . . . second cousin?" Her eyes flash back to me, crinkling with uncertainty.

"Former roommate," I remind her gently.

"Right. Sorry. Damn pregnancy brain." She knocks against her head with her knuckles, making a hollow sound with her tongue.

It gets a chuckle out of Brett, who lifts his girl-friend's hand to his lips and kisses her knuckles. "Pregnancy brain or not, she's still the smartest person I know," he says, sending a flush of pink creeping across Beth's cheeks.

"Oh, stop it, you." She giggles, swatting his arm playfully.

Something tells me that she does not, in fact, want him to stop it.

If there were any question as to whether this little bundle of joy would bring Connor and Beth back together in any serious way, this little interaction just answered it. Beth is enamored with this Brett guy, who is lanky and blond and obviously no stranger to the lovey-dovey stuff. Pretty much everything that Connor is not.

It looks like this little girl is going to have two very different dads. But I think that's a good thing. *Right?*

"There you are, dude." Connor emerges from the kitchen with a craft brew in each hand, handing one bottle to me and clinking the other against it. "Thought you'd fallen into a pothole or something."

"Nah, just running a bit late. Your sister was really taking her time with that cake of yours."

I glance over to the couch, where Penelope is sitting with some of the girls, laughing along to whatever story Maren is telling. *God*, that laugh is infectious. I can't help but smile every time I hear it. She must feel my gaze on her, because her blue eyes meet mine moments later. When she shoots me a wink, it sends my heart on overdrive. It's still a little hard to believe that beautiful woman is all mine.

"Quit staring at her, bro." Connor slugs me in the shoulder, nearly causing me to spill my beer all over his nice clean carpet. "Start looking at a woman like that and next thing you know, you're moving out to the suburbs at the start of her third trimester."

Beth and I both roll our eyes at that remark.

Part of me wants to reassure him that, despite me not having purchased a box of condoms since Penelope and I started dating, his sister takes a small white pill once a day to make sure we don't go down that road anytime soon. But I suspect that might be a bit more information than he'd like to hear about our relationship. He may be cool with us being together, but I don't want to press my luck.

If I'm being completely honest, Penelope carrying my baby is an idea that should scare me. I've never been sure I even wanted kids. But for some reason, the idea of her round and full with my baby doesn't scare me at all. In fact, it sends a rush of heat and emotions galloping through me that I don't have time to dissect right now.

Because across the room, a resonant clinking sound pulls everyone's attention over to the gift table. It's Scarlett, tapping a fork against a half-full champagne flute.

"Sorry to interrupt, everyone, but may I suggest we open presents?" She shifts her weight. "I don't want to make it all about me, but I have to be back in the city for work by five."

"Boo! Work!" Penelope shouts, getting a laugh from the group, Scarlett included.

"I second that," she says with a chuckle, "but that's the event-planner lifestyle, working weekends and all that jazz."

"Speaking of event planners," I say, hoisting my beer in the air. "Let's hear it for Penelope for planning this shower."

"To Penelope!" Connor says, raising his beer with mine. Soon, the air is filled with everyone's drink of choice, from craft beers to cocktails, right down to Beth's nonalcoholic seltzer.

Penelope's cheeks turn the sweetest shade of pink as she sips her champagne, humbly accepting the praise. She deserves every bit of it for how well this baby shower turned out. None of those dreaded *smell the diaper* or *guess the baby's weight* games. Just the warm, fuzzy feeling that can only come from the perfect combination of good friends and good food.

"So, presents?" Scarlett suggests again, motioning for everyone to take a seat.

Beth seems game with this idea, and she joins Connor in one of the two armchairs by the fireplace. We all refill our drinks and settle in, and Maren graciously sacrifices her spot on the couch so I can sit next to Penelope.

"We were just chatting about what a freaking gorgeous couple the two of you are," Maren says as she cozies up to Hayes on the leather loveseat. "The four of us should totally go on a double date sometime soon."

Scarlett groans, folding her arms over her chest as she sinks into the couch next to me. "Thank you so much for the painful reminder of my singleness. I'd be double-dating a double shot of vodka if I didn't have to work in three hours."

"Everyone knows you're dating your job, Scar," Maren reminds her.

"Sure, sure," Scarlett says with an eye roll. "And Lord knows I'll be getting plenty of action from my job tonight."

"Would you rather have no job at all?" Penelope leans over me to wiggle her eyebrows at Scarlett. "Because I would happily trade places with you, if you want."

"Oops, sorry. My bad." Scarlett cringes with embarrassment, forcing a painful, apologetic smile.

"Any luck on the job-search front, girl?"

Penelope shakes her head. "I've sent out a few résumés, but I haven't heard back yet. Keep your fingers crossed for me. My emergency fund is getting low."

"You wouldn't have to worry about rent if you lived with me," I murmur into her ear.

She just laughs and plants a quick kiss on my cheek. "Two more months on my lease," she reminds me. "Then I'll move in with you. I promise."

"And I promise that you have big roommate shoes to fill." Connor, who apparently has the listening skills of a bat, laughs as he pretends to brush dust off his shoulders. "I'm just saying, I was pretty much the best roomie of all time."

"You were the loudest roomie of all time," I mumble just loud enough for Penelope to hear, and she covers her ears with a laugh. I'm sure she doesn't want to hear about her brother's frequent, noisy weekend extracurriculars.

"Okay, seriously, folks." Scarlett taps her invisible watch with one manicured pink fingernail. "Enough chitchat. The clock is ticking. Let's get these presents open!"

For the next half hour, Beth and Connor take

turns peeling pink and white wrapping paper off of boxes and wrangling things out of gift bags, unveiling identical pairs of nearly everything on their joint baby registry. Two high chairs, two baby monitors, two gift cards with enough money for a year's supply of diapers.

Brett is sitting nearby with his phone, taking pictures and jotting down who gifted what for thank-you-note purposes.

I was expecting an element of awkwardness to this whole party, but all three of them just look so happy. So ready to be parents, each in their own different, nontraditional way. Maybe it wasn't in Connor's plan to be a dad just yet, but it looks like things are really going to work out for the best.

With the presents open and the cake cut and served, Scarlett makes her rounds, congratulating the parents-to-be and hugging everyone good-bye. When she makes it over to Penelope, she pulls her into an extra-tight hug, one hand still wrapped around her waist as she turns to me.

"So, *Wolfgang*," she says, her voice is stern.

I shudder at the use of my full name, even though I know she's just using it to be dramatic. "Yes?"

"Last I talked to my best friend, Penelope, she

said you were in the business of making clean get-aways. You promise you're not going to run away on her this time?"

My brow crinkles, and then it registers. Penelope must have talked to her after my little *sprint out of the kitchen in the middle of a make-out* incident. Not my best look, but I've come a long damn way since then.

"I'm not going anywhere," I say firmly. "No more running off, no more hot and cold. Your best friend is in good hands."

"She'd better be," Scarlett says, giving me a vicious death glare that quickly fades to a bubbly laugh. "Oh, I'm just kidding. You two are a perfect match."

She pulls me in for a hug, then hugs Penelope again before she finally heads for the door.

"I'm so sorry about that." Penelope laces her fingers tight with mine, giving my hand a quick squeeze.

I shake my head and squeeze back. "Don't be. Your friends are just looking out for you. If I need to tell them a thousand times that I'm not going anywhere, I will."

She chuckles softly, rolling her eyes. "You

don't have to do that, Wolfie."

"You're right." I shrug. "I'll just prove it instead."

And I will prove it. Every second of every day. Because that's what you do when you find a once-in-a-lifetime girl like Penelope Blake.

Epilogue

PENELOPE

"**G**ood morning, Penelope!"

My coworker Reagan waves to me from her cubicle as I walk past her on my way to my corner desk. I wiggle my fingers back, shooting her the brightest smile I can muster at seven in the morning. Because despite all my efforts, I'm still not a morning person.

It never fails to surprise me how early she gets to the office every day, and how she manages to have so much energy before she's even finished her coffee. Still, her cheerful smile is the best way to start a busy workday. Which, according to the very full calendar on my phone, today is shaping up to be.

"Morning, Reagan. Happy Friday."

I shrug out of my wool pea coat and hang it on the hook next to my desk, then slip out of my snow boots and swap them for the sensible flats I have tucked in my purse, completing my transformation from Commuting Penelope to Office Penelope.

I couldn't have asked for a better location for my new place of employment—just a few blocks from a Brown Line stop. I don't have to be out in the cold for too long, and the building tucked back just far enough from the busiest part of Michigan Avenue that I don't have to push past too many tourists on my commute. As a bonus, the window next to my desk provides a million-dollar view of Millennium Park, which feels like a sign that I've officially made it in Chicago.

"You ready for our eight a.m. call?" Reagan asks, her hazel eyes peering up at me from over the side of her cubicle.

This call is the reason I'm here a little early this morning. I wanted to make sure I was prepped.

"As ready as I can be to talk shop with the president of a Fortune 500 company," I say with a laugh. "But actually, I spent almost three hours going over their annual report last night. I'll send you my notes."

I turn on my computer and forward her the document, waiting for the ping from her cubicle that tells me she's received it.

"Wow, this is impressive," Reagan says. "They're going to be thrilled with this work."

I can't help the proud smile that breaks out on my face.

What can I say? Going above and beyond is sort of my thing. I've made that perfectly clear in the short few weeks I've been working for the Glenbury Group. And by the way my boss keeps whispering about upward mobility around me, I'd say it's paying off in a major way.

After a quick scan through my inbox and a refresher on the correspondence we've had with this client since last week, I roll my chair back from my desk, glancing at my watch.

"I think I'm going to swing by the cafe in the lobby for a latte," I say. "Do you want anything, Reagan?"

Before I can stand up, the top of her head pops up over her cubicle wall, her hazel eyes doubling in size. "Wait! I almost forgot. Stay put for just one second, okay?" She scurries off to the kitchen, returning moments later with a beverage carrier holding two extra-large caramel-colored iced coffees. "Ta-da! Happy one month working at the firm!"

I laugh, shaking my head in disbelief as I push to my feet. "You didn't have to do that. It's just a month, not a birthday or something."

She lifts a shoulder, holding the tray out to me. "I know it's silly, but I figured we should take whatever little celebrations life gives us, right? Plus, since we're both iced vanilla latte girls, it just felt right."

"You're crazy." I laugh, although whether she's sane or not doesn't change the fact that I could definitely use the caffeine. I shimmy a cup from its spot in the beverage carrier and take a slow sip from the straw. "You're the greatest. How do you keep track of stuff like this?"

"I'm good with dates, I guess. Plus, I put a note in my calendar so I wouldn't forget. I feel like you need things to celebrate to get you through a Midwest winter, you know?"

I laugh in agreement. "That's for sure. And by the way, thank you for supporting the lifestyle of drinking iced coffee, even in the winter."

"It's *always* iced coffee season," she says with the same gravity she brings to the most important client meetings. "Thank God we both know that."

It's so nice to have a coworker I'm not going to be constantly competing with. Reagan is a couple years older than me, but she's made it clear she's perfectly happy being an office assistant for now. When the time comes and she's interested in more responsibility, I vow to never be like that jerk Spencer. I'll show her the ropes, teach her everything I've learned in this role, and help her get any promotion she desires.

I settle back in at my desk, sipping happily on my iced latte as I reply to a few quick client emails, only to be distracted moments later when my computer pings with an instant message. It's from Wolfie, and just seeing his name appear on my screen puts a fluttery feeling deep in my chest.

We've been official for almost two months now, but that new-love feeling still hasn't worn off, and my fingers are crossed that it never will. I glance at the time in the corner of my screen—okay, I have a couple of minutes to chat before this meeting. Let's make it count.

When I open the message, I'm surprised to see it's really not a message at all. Just a link to a website with a URL I don't recognize. For a second, I'm suspicious, but the link doesn't appear to be spam or anything.

With a double-click, I'm whisked off to a real estate page boasting lots of bright, airy pictures of a two-bedroom condo for sale, right on the lake. I swipe through the pictures, impressed by the rich brown hardwood floors and the modern kitchen appliances.

When I get to the pictures of the floor-to-ceiling windows overlooking the sparkling blue lake, my jaw almost hits my keyboard. It's gorgeous, but I'm not really sure why he's sending it to me.

We haven't discussed the whole moving-in-together thing since we made our relationship official, and even then, I thought the condo daydream was a few more years down the line. Then again, my lease is ending pretty soon. It's about time for us to be more serious about what comes next.

This condo is way out of my price range, but I know Wolfie makes a great living with Frisky Business. My brother hasn't exactly been shy about getting my advice about the business or showing me the books over the years. All the partners have been making seven figures for a while now.

My fingers fly across my keyboard, typing out a quick response.

Are you thinking about buying this place?

Almost instantly, my computer pings with Wolfie's reply.

I'm looking at it. If you don't like it, there are a few others I have in mind. I think any of them could be excellent for our first home together.

There's that fluttery feeling in my chest again.

I reopen the website and take another more serious look at the listing, trying to imagine myself inside each beautiful, spacious room. Ideas start rushing to my head quicker than I can talk myself down from my daydream. We could put the couch there, the kitchen table here. The second bedroom would be for guests, with a crib ready for Connor's baby girl when they visit.

It all seems too good to be true.

And then there's the very best part—the thought of coming home to Wolfie at the end of every day.

It's beautiful. Even the location is perfect. But isn't it a little fast for us to share a mortgage?

His response makes my head swim.

Then I'll buy it and you can live with me, rent-free. It'll be half yours anyway once there's a ring on your finger.

This time, the butterflies aren't just in my chest.

They're in my stomach, and my fingertips, and even my freaking armpits. I can't believe this man sometimes.

You're too good to be true, you know that? And I'm helping with the payments!

No way. You know I come with baggage. I'm just lucky enough to have a girl who sees past it.

When I don't respond right away, he messages me again.

The realtor can get us in for a showing tonight, if you're free after work.

Tonight? Already? I didn't know this would move so fast. This all feels so crazy.

I never expected things to move so quickly with Wolfie, but much to my surprise, I'm not afraid. Just excited. Sometimes life moves a little faster than we could have planned, and all you can do is throw your arms up and enjoy the ride.

Opening my calendar again, I scroll through the back-to-back meetings and phone calls filling my day. It might be a race against the clock, but I think I can get out of here by six, if I focus. Starting, like, now.

Tonight sounds perfect. Meet me at the office after work? Six o'clock?

Perfect. Just like you. I love you.

I bask in the glow of those last two words for a good long moment. Wolfie loves me. I'll never get tired of hearing it. Or reading it on a screen, in this case.

Either way, those words leave a floaty feeling in my belly that even the most exhausting of workdays can't take away.

By the time six o'clock rolls around, I should be completely drained, but the excitement of seeing this condo with him has me riding a high.

When Wolfie texts me that he's arrived, I slip back into my snow boots and take the elevator down to the lobby, where he's seated on one of the black leather couches near reception. Waiting patiently for me, he scrolls through his phone, just like I waited patiently for him, all those years and diary entries ago. But this reality is far better than anything I ever could have put on paper.

I walk toward him, and when he sees me, his gray eyes light up like he just spotted his favorite thing in the world. I love those expressive eyes, the ones that always shine when they lock with mine. Even at the end of a long workweek in the dead of winter, one look from him could warm me up from the inside faster than a shot of bourbon.

He shoves up from the couch, gathering me in his arms for a quick kiss hello. His lips are as soft and sweet as ever, although a little cold from the winter weather. But the heat in his gaze when he pulls back is absolutely undeniable.

"Hi, gorgeous," he murmurs. "Ready to check out our future home?"

I roll my eyes and give his shoulder a pat. "Don't get ahead of yourself, babe. It's a showing, not a closing. How was work?"

"Good," he says with a nod. "And you?"

"Good. Long, but good. I'm starving, though. Do we have time to pick up a snack on our way to the showing?"

His laugh is a low cackle, barely audible through the lobby noise. "Way ahead of you, babe.

I picked up dinner on the way here. It's out in the car, if you don't mind using your lap as a table."

My stomach answers for me with a grumble. "Um, that's a yes," I say with a blush, lacing my gloved fingers through his and following him toward the revolving doors. "What's on the menu?"

"Pasta," he says, his smile wider than a city block. "Just like our first date. When you cooked for me."

I smile at the memory. That was the start of us . . . back when I was so unsure how it would all unfold, but couldn't stop myself from falling hard and fast.

It's been an incredible ride, and I wouldn't change any of it for a single second.

I hope you enjoyed Wolfie's story. Up next in this series is Connor's story in *The Stud Next Door*. Turn the page for a sneak preview!

What to Read Next

THE NEXT DOOR
One

CONNOR

Sunlight pours onto the front porch of the three-bedroom home I bought a few months ago. I gave up my apartment in the city for a suburban zip code, a lawn I don't have time to mow, and nosy neighbors who want to know why my baby's mom isn't in the picture.

It's . . . a lot.

But at this moment, lawn mowers and property taxes are the least of my concerns.

The stress I've been under for the last few months, ever since my daughter was born, has been beaten into temporary submission by the warmth of the sunshine, good company, and the cold beer in my hand. It still lurks just below the surface, in the tension in my shoulders, in the dark thoughts that linger, but for now at least, I'm relatively at ease. Summer has finally come to Chicago, and I'm parked in a lawn chair on my porch with three of my best friends.

"Just like old times. Right, man?" Hayes leans back in his chair, kicking his feet up onto the brick ledge.

Hayes is the easygoing one, always able to put people at ease. I used to be that way. Friendly, fun-loving. Always down for a good time. Now it's a mixed bag. The stress of becoming a single father has done a number on me, and I'm still fighting for breath on what feels like a sinking ship at times.

"Something like that," I murmur, lifting the bottle to my lips for a sip. The beer goes down with a bite, hoppy and full-bodied.

To my left, Wolfie grunts his approval. In contrast to Hayes, Wolfie is a bit of a handful. Complicated, but loyal. Unpredictably moody, yet reliable. Although his foul moods have improved drastically since he started dating my younger sister—a story that I have no intention of getting into right now.

"Thanks for the beer, man," I say, raising my beverage in Caleb's direction.

"Fuck yeah. Anytime," he says before downing what I can only assume is half of his beer and releasing an enormous belch.

Caleb is a bit of a wild child. I keep waiting for the guy to grow up, but so far, that hasn't happened. He's still the same shamelessly immature guy I met in college.

"Chill, man," Hayes whispers, nodding in my direction. "Boys' night isn't just for the *boys* anymore."

Ah. That's my cue to acknowledge that "one of these things is not like the other." The reason I've been working from home for the past two months. The elephant in the room that's less of an elephant and more of a . . . well, a newborn baby.

A baby girl named Marley who has my eyes and my ex's creamy skin.

"Oh, come on. She's dead asleep." Caleb leans forward in his chair. "Hey, Marley! Maaarley. Marzipan!"

My two-month-old daughter doesn't wake, nestled peacefully against my chest, her plump little fist clutching my T-shirt.

We all take a moment to watch the rise and fall of her back, the cutest little poop-and-puke machine you ever did see. Even when she's pooping and puking, she's the most beautiful thing in the world, and you can fight me on that. I'll die on that hill.

"How's she been?" Wolfie asks, tipping his chin toward the sleeping baby with a deep line etched between his brows.

I smile. I've missed my old roommate's perpetual frown.

Paternity leave has been . . . interesting. A bit isolating, but I'm starting to realize it doesn't have to be that way.

"Good. She's good." It isn't a lie. Marley is a good baby, usually low maintenance with only the occasional meltdown. Kind of like her dad.

"How about you?" Hayes frowns as he studies me.

Damn, I must look as exhausted as I feel.

"I'm alive." I chuckle, but the humor in my voice sounds forced. That's a new one for me.

"You'll feel better once you're back." Caleb nods sagely, as if my returning to work will somehow restore the balance of the universe.

"*If* I come back," I remind them, only half joking.

My partners graciously gave me six weeks of

paid paternity leave, with a little leeway in the budget to sneak in another week or two.

Together, my friends and I own a sex toy business named Frisky Business, both an ecofriendly line of toys that we manufacture, as well as a retail store in the heart of Chicago. Despite the shop being a second home to me for years, I haven't set foot in the place in six weeks, and part of me can't picture myself going back. At least, not without some reliable child care, which has been hard to come by.

"What about the day cares you were researching?" Wolfie asks, and I can see him crunching the numbers in his head.

I'm well aware that Frisky Business can't afford to keep me on paternity leave for much longer. It's already been two months.

"No luck. Did you know there's a government website where you can look up safety violations and infractions of any licensed day care? It's terrifying. All of the day cares within a five-mile radius have too many accident reports to even count."

"Shit, seriously? Well, what about Beth?" Hayes asks.

Ah, yes. Beth. Part-time mother of my child, full-time med-school student alongside her med-school-student boyfriend.

They certainly don't have the time to care for a child 24/7. We share joint custody, but a lot has been falling on me lately, not that I'm complaining. I love spending time with Marley, and I want Beth to be able to build her career. She's a good mom, juggling school, a new relationship, and Marley with relative ease.

"When she finishes her residency next year, she'll have more time to care for Marley. For now, she and Brett have her two days of the week. Beth wants more, but she can't quite swing it right now."

The guys nod, trying to understand this new life I've found myself living.

One day at a time . . .

Let's rewind. Thirteen months ago, I was happily single without a care in the world. The only unknown in my life was the familiar and somewhat amusing panic of waking up next to a woman whose name I couldn't remember. Back then, I was going on a minimum of three dates per week, some of which ended with a satisfying hookup with whichever lucky lady could keep up with me.

My love-for-life dial was cranked up to 100 and locked into place with superglue. Nothing was gonna slow me down.

Of course, all that changed with a phone call from my former friends-with-benefits. Beth was busy becoming a doctor, and neither of us had time for a relationship. But Netflix and chilling became our thing for a couple of months last year, until those two little pink lines changed everything. Beth was carrying my baby, despite the precautions we'd taken.

But even with the massive overhaul of my social life, life is better with Marley, on all counts. She's given me purpose, a word I thought was only reserved for the kind of people who go on mission trips to Guatemala twice a year.

Nowadays, I'm more than just Connor Blake, the bachelor. More than co-owner of Chicago's number one sex toy shop.

I'm a dad.

When I come to, I realize I've been droning on about day cares for give or take ten minutes. Even Wolfie's sharp eyes are starting to glaze over.

"In summary," I mutter, "finding a good day care in this neighborhood is a bitch."

"Why don't you just get a nanny?" Caleb says, cracking open a second beer. "I had the best nanny growing up. She still comes to my family's Christmas party each year."

"Probably 'cause you still need supervision." I sneer at him, relishing the opportunity to give him a hard time.

But before Caleb can get a word out, Hayes cuts in.

"Where do you even find a nanny?"

"I'm sure there are databases for nannies," Wolfie says, ever the pragmatic one.

"I don't want to pick some random person off the internet, guys. If I get a nanny, they'd be alone in my home for the majority of the day. I'd need to trust them."

"Do you have anything valuable to steal?"

It's Caleb's turn to give me shit, and damn, does it feel like we're back in the shop. With a sleeping baby on my chest, I can't smack him upside the head like I normally would. I'll make up for it by teaching Marley to kick Uncle Caleb in the shins every chance she gets.

"Other than his kid?" Hayes chuckles, shaking his head.

Never too proud for a pissing contest, I'm about to tell him exactly how much I paid for my high-end espresso machine when a moving truck rolls to a halt in front of my neighbor's house. The Wilkes have lived in that house for over two decades as happily retired empty nesters. I've only met them a couple of times, but the old couple have grown on me. I wonder if something happened. They never mentioned moving out.

Hayes, Wolfie, and Caleb must sense my curiosity, because the conversation stills as we wait to see who steps out of the truck.

I hear the door slam and the soft padding of feet before I know who they belong to. When the driver comes into view to lift the roll-up door, I can't help but do a double-take because the girl is unbelievably gorgeous.

She's young, around our age, with thick brown hair pulled back in a long, unruly ponytail. Wearing sneakers, shorts, and a loose-fitting T-shirt, she looks like any twenty-something on moving day. She climbs up into the truck easily, clearly stronger than she looks, and disappears into a sea of cardboard boxes.

"Do your neighbors have a hot daughter?" Caleb asks, standing to get a better look.

"Will you sit down?" Wolfie sighs, aging with every second that Caleb does anything immature.

For the first time in a while, I'm kind of with Caleb on this one. I'm curious.

"Just sons, as far as I know," I murmur.

When she reappears, I see her face for the first time. She's flushed, but not just with the summer heat. *She's excited.* And excitement looks really damn good on her.

"Jessa!"

We all turn to see Mr. and Mrs. Wilkes waving to her from their porch with wide, friendly smiles. The woman we now know as Jessa sets a box down on the edge of the truck bed and hops down with a wave. She jogs over to them, giving Mr. Wilkes a hearty handshake and Mrs. Wilkes a quick hug. I can't hear their conversation, but I get the impression they're meeting for the first time.

"All right, I'm bored." Caleb sighs, plopping back down in his chair. "Anyone want another beer? Or am I supposed to finish this twelve-pack all by myself?"

I peer down at Marley, who is squirming unhappily, her bleary little eyes opening and closing. I guess nap time is over.

Out of the corner of my eye, I see Jessa's box tilting over the lip of the truck bed, about to topple. Instinctively, I jump to my feet, jostling the already grumpy baby. The box falls, Marley wails, Jessa and the Wilkes turn, and suddenly everyone's eyes are on me.

"Fuck," I mutter under my breath. "It's okay, Marley. It's okay." I pat her back softly, but it's like comforting a fire alarm. I turn to the guys. "Would someone go help her with that box?"

Caleb and Wolfie spring into action as Hayes leans across the brick ledge toward the neighbors with an apologetic smile. "Sorry for the commotion, folks. Can we help you out?"

"Oh, that's all right. It wasn't fragile stuff. Don't worry about it," Jessa calls back, her voice clear and cordial.

But Caleb and Wolfie are already unpacking the truck, box by box.

"Really, it's okay," she says, trying to intercept Wolfie on his trajectory to the Wilkes's front porch. One look at him in the zone, and Jessa steps aside, her eyes wide and a timid smile on her lips. "Well, thanks, um . . ."

"Wolfie's the scary one. That idiot's Caleb," Hayes says, waving off her concern. "Best to just let them do their thing. They've already got an assembly line going."

And they do. Caleb stands in the truck, passing down boxes as Wolfie carries them toward the house, where Mr. and Mrs. Wilkes direct him inside.

You'd better believe that I'd be right there with them if I didn't have a screaming baby in my arms. Marley's eyes are scrunched tightly closed, tears trailing down her pink cheeks.

I try rocking her. I try bouncing her.

Is she crying because she's tired? Hungry? Scared? I never fucking know.

In the ear that isn't already deaf, I hear Hayes making polite conversation.

"That's my buddy Connor's house." He points in my direction. "He's the normal one. I'm Hayes, by the way. Where are you coming from?"

"Oh, I'm Jessa. Nice to meet you. I'm from a couple hours east of here. Well, east is the lake. Southeast. I'm from Indiana." She laughs, somehow pulling off awkward and sweet at the same time.

Unable to take my eyes off of her, I ask, "What brings you to Chicago?" Instantly, I regret drawing attention to myself.

Yes, let's all look at the sad son of a bitch who has no idea how to calm his distraught baby.

I shift Marley's weight in my arms, hoping a new position will help. It doesn't.

I don't even hear Jessa's answer to my question, as much as I'd like to. While Jessa and Hayes continue making small talk, I pace back and forth, trying to soothe Marley. I wish I knew what was wrong so I could fix it. She does this once in a while, and I've yet to figure it out.

"How old is she?"

I turn to see Jessa walking up the steps, a warm smile on her lips. She's close enough now that I can fully take in her features—light blue eyes, long lashes, and dozens of pretty freckles dotting her nose and cheeks. *The neighbor girl is cute as hell.*

"Uh, two months," I say, my tone harsher than I'd like it to be. *Why the fuck am I nervous?*

"The best months." Jessa nods, clasping her hands in front of her heart.

There's something so warm about this girl. It's like it comes off her in waves. I have to step back to keep from sweating. But she follows me, her arms outstretched.

What the . . .

"May I?"

My gaze darts over to where Hayes is standing, but he offers me nothing but a useless shrug.

"Sure," I mutter, allowing Jessa to step into the same square footage as me. The smell of her is intoxicating, sweet and floral, a mixture of shampoo and something decidedly feminine.

Her hands brush against my arms as she scoops Marley into hers. My heart nearly stops when she flips Marley over, my dad-brain warning me of danger. But when Jessa starts massaging Marley's back, the baby stops crying immediately.

"Gas bubbles," Jessa says, all smiles, and Marley sighs happily.

I'm damn near shocked speechless.

"Holy baby whisperer," Hayes blurts, his eyes wide.

I'm glad to see I'm not the only one blown away.

"How did you do that?" I ask, aware of how dumb I sound. I don't even care. She's amazing.

"I'm the oldest of six. I can just tell," she says, her nose scrunching up adorably in unison with her shrug.

Humble too? Be still my cold, dead heart.

"Are you free for a nannying job?" Hayes asks, looking more at me than Jessa.

I shoot him a glare and he glares back, his eyes saying, *What? You need a nanny, dude.*

"Oh," she says with a laugh. "I don't know. I've never been a nanny before."

She carefully adjusts Marley so that she's supported comfortably. An unfamiliar warmth floods through my chest at the sight of my baby girl in Jessa's careful embrace.

"I guess I do need a part-time job," she says more to herself than to me. "What's her name?"

"Marley," I say, hardly recognizing my own voice.

"Marley!" She coos, nuzzling her nose against my daughter's soft hair. "The perfect name."

Hayes cuts in. "And he's Connor. Could you give him your number?" He means well, but this recruitment is downright aggressive. And annoying.

Shaking my head, I say, "You don't have to—"

"No, I don't mind. I'll put it in your phone. Trade you."

With a moment's hesitation, I pull out my

phone, and Jessa and I swap baby and device with minimal fumbling.

As her quick fingers type her number into my phone, her thumb ring catches my eye. It's delicate and feminine, a simple band wrapped around a small amber jewel. Did her boyfriend give that to her?

"Here you go. Nice to meet you, Connor," she murmurs, her long eyelashes casting shadows on her rosy cheeks. When she gives my phone back to me, our fingers brush with an electric shock.

"Sorry!" she says. "Static electricity."

"All good." I chuckle, smiling sincerely for the first time in weeks. *Nice to meet you too, Jessa.*

As the sun begins its descent, Jessa and the Wilkes leave to return the moving truck in a two-vehicle caravan. Marley is fast asleep in the crook of my arm. The guys are finishing off their final beers for the evening, and I'm utterly exhausted.

"Hire that girl," Hayes says firmly, clapping me on the shoulder. "You don't have to do it all by yourself. You need the help."

"Come on," I say with a scoff. "You heard her. She has no experience."

He shrugs. "Well, she knew how to get Marley

to stop crying. She seemed pretty experienced to me."

I release a slow sigh. "I'll think about it. Now, get out of here so I can put Marley down for the night."

"Let's leave the man alone," Wolfie says quickly. He can always sense when it's time to leave.

The guys say their good-byes, and before I know it, I'm alone again.

I miss having Wolfie as a roommate more than I'd like to admit, but we're both better off this way. No need to have both of us losing sleep at night, effectively knocking down Frisky Business's production levels by half. Besides, the man's in love, and with my sister, no less. Our friendship needed some space.

After kicking off my shoes, I heat up some leftovers and carry my plate and Marley into the living room. After I settle the baby into her body pillow on the couch beside me, I grab my food and the remote.

This is my favorite part of the day. I've worked hard to get Marley on a schedule. I know that I'll have to adjust it as she gets older, but for now, she crashes by seven, so this quiet time we get together before bed is pretty sweet. As I eat, she blinks up at me and listens to my predictions about Chicago's hockey team this season.

"Nystrom's looking good this year," I say, glancing at Marley.

She stretches her arms over her head and lets out a yawn. I chuckle and take another bite of my food.

I hope we can share quiet moments like this as she grows. Eating pizza. Watching the game. Maybe even a little trash-talking about the opposing team. The idea of a precocious teenager with Beth's blue eyes and my dark hair sharing in some smack talk about any team who's *not* Chicago brings a smile to my face.

By the time I've finished eating, Marley's already asleep.

I carry her to her bedroom where her crib and changing station live. I've become something of an expert in changing diapers quickly and without any fuss.

Marley is still sound asleep when I lay her down on the soft mattress pad of her crib. In these moments, I don't feel like an actor performing the role of father. I *am* her father.

I watch her sleep, all soft sighs and tiny grasping fingers.

I love this little girl so damn much.

The soft look on Jessa's face when she held Marley . . . it was like she loved her too. Like she was her own. I shake off the thought, recognizing it for what it is: my dad-brain desperately looking for a mate to help rear my child.

As attracted as I am to Jessa, I can't let my imagination get the better of me. Even so, I can admire her bright blue eyes and distinct freckles. I can fantasize about her full lips, how they might feel under my fingers, under my own lips.

She's beautiful, and if I weren't emotionally unavailable, I wouldn't have questioned pursuing her. The reality is that I can't afford any distractions right now. Not when a tiny life depends on my full attention.

You need the help.

Hayes may have a point. I can't stay holed up in my house as a full-time dad forever. I have to take breaks, I have to have fun, and most importantly—I have to get back to work.

Sitting on the edge of my bed, I tap out a text before I can psych myself out.

If you're interested in that nanny position, let's talk. Would you be free for a
                                chat tomorrow?

I press SEND. The message is direct and professional, with no indication of exactly how much
I'm attracted to Jessa. And if I have any control
over my libido, she'll never know.

Acknowledgments

Thank you so much, lovely readers! You are the reason I get to continue bringing my stories to life, and I truly hope you enjoyed this one as much as I enjoyed getting to tell it. Up next in this series is Connor's story in *The Stud Next Door*.

A huge amount of gratitude is owed to my lovely assistant, Alyssa; to my editors Rachel and Pam; to my agent, Jane; and to my audio production team. You're all truly outstanding at what you do. And to my sweet little family . . . I couldn't do it without you.

Get Two Free Books

Sign up for my newsletter and I'll automatically send you two free books.

www.kendallryanbooks.com/newsletter

Follow Kendall

Website

www.kendallryanbooks.com

Facebook

www.facebook.com/kendallryanbooks

Twitter

www.twitter.com/kendallryan1

Instagram

www.instagram.com/kendallryan1

Newsletter

www.kendallryanbooks.com/newsletter/

Other Books By Kendall Ryan

Unravel Me

Filthy Beautiful Lies Series

The Room Mate

The Play Mate

The House Mate

Screwed

The Fix Up

Dirty Little Secret

xo, Zach

Baby Daddy

Tempting Little Tease

Bro Code

Love Machine

Flirting with Forever

Dear Jane

Only for Tonight

Boyfriend for Hire

The Two-Week Arrangement

For a complete list of Kendall's books, visit:

www.kendallryanbooks.com/all-books/

Printed in Great Britain
by Amazon

60968719R00201